THE GREAT CENTURIES OF PAINTING

COLLECTION PLANNED AND DIRECTED BY

ALBERT SKIRA

Translated by M. E. Stanley and Stuart Gilbert

Copyright 1952, by Editions Albert Skira, Geneva (Switzerland)

PRINTED IN SWITZERLAND

THE GREAT CENTURIES OF PAINTING

ETRUSCAN PAINTING

TEXT BY MASSIMO PALLOTTINO
Professor at the University of Rome

The colorplate of the title page :
Crouching Bull. Tomb of the Bulls, Tarquinii.

ETRUSCAN PAINTING

AN INTRODUCTION TO THE PICTORIAL ART OF THE ETRUSCANS

I

THE PRIMITIVES: FROM ORIENTAL INFLUENCES
TO THE IONICO-ETRUSCAN PERIOD
(SIXTH CENTURY B.C.)

BOCCANERA SLABS · TOMB OF THE BULLS
CAMPANA SLABS · TOMB OF THE AUGURS
TOMB OF THE LIONESSES · TOMB OF HUNTING AND FISHING
TOMB OF THE BACCHANTS · TOMB OF THE BARON

II

THE MASTERS OF THE SEVERE STYLE
(FIFTH CENTURY B.C.)

TOMB OF THE CHARIOTS
TOMB OF THE MONKEY · TOMB OF THE LEOPARDS
TOMB OF THE TRICLINIUM · TOMB OF THE FUNERAL COUCH
FRANCESCA GIUSTINIANI TOMB

III

CLASSICAL INFLUENCES
(FOURTH CENTURY B.C.)

SARCOPHAGUS OF THE AMAZONS · GOLINI TOMB
TOMB OF ORCUS (EARLIER CHAMBER)

IV

THE PAINTING OF THE HELLENISTIC PERIOD
(THIRD-FIRST CENTURY B.C.)

TOMB OF THE SHIELDS · TOMB OF ORCUS (LATER CHAMBER)
FRANÇOIS TOMB · TOMB OF THE TYPHON

Whereas Etruscan sculpture, bronzes and vases are well known to art lovers and connoisseurs in general, the same cannot be said of the paintings with which this mysterious people adorned their funerary monuments. The relatively few illustrations of Etruscan pictorial art that have hitherto been available, consisting only of drawings or watercolor sketches after the originals, or black-and-white photographs, could give only a partial, fragmentary conception of what this strange art really is. In this volume, with its 64 illustrations, these paintings, reproduced by the direct color-separation process, will be shown for the first time in their original colors and presented as an organic whole. The illuminating commentaries accompanying the color-plates and the ample documentation will be, we believe, of the highest interest for the general public and art critics alike, and will facilitate researches into this fascinating and intriguing art manifestation of the ancient world. The publication of this book has been rendered possible by the kind permission given to reproduce these paintings by the Direzione Generale delle Antichità e Belle Arti of the Italian Ministry of Public Instruction and the affiliated departments of the Soprintendenze alle Antichità at Rome (Southern Etruria) and at Florence; by the Directorates of the British Museum, London, and the Louvre, Paris; by the members of the Princely House of Torlonia, Rome (for the pictures from the François Tomb). To all the publisher tenders his very grateful thanks.

A. S.

HAND AND BIRD, DETAIL. TOMB OF THE AUGURS, TARQUINII.

ETRUSCAN PAINTING

AN INTRODUCTION TO THE PICTORIAL ART OF THE ETRUSCANS

ANCIENT Etruria has bequeathed to us a great number of paintings, for the most part brought to light during the archaeological researches of the last two hundred years, and these rank amongst the most interesting and suggestive phenomena of all ancient art, not to say of the whole world's art.

We have here, in fact, the first chapter of the history of Italian painting; and it is an interesting point that the pictorial genius of the Italic peoples should have manifested itself originally in that selfsame part of Italy, around the Tiber and Arno, which fifteen centuries later was to be the scene of the noblest pictorial achievements of the late Middle Ages and the Tuscan Renaissance. But Etruscan painting is also a precious and in a sense unique source of information for the understanding of ancient art. It constitutes the only extant group of large-scale paintings of the classical world before the Roman period. For what we have here is not secondary decorative work, productions of mere artisans or pale imitations of loftier creations now lost for ever. Far otherwise, these are works of high stylistic achievement, at once fertile in suggestions and full of fascination for the art historian and for the connoisseur. What is more, these pictures have an inestimable documentary value, since they constantly aim at concrete, spontaneous, detailed renderings of reality, and thus give us an insight into the mentality of the Etruscan people and, by extension, into the civilization of ancient Italy.

The Etruscans, as is well known, played a leading part in the history of Primitive Italy before its conquest and unification by the Romans. They formed a homogeneous nation on the Tyrrhenian side of Central Italy, occupying a region corresponding to

Upper Latium and present-day Tuscany. The archaeological and linguistic records of their national history relate to a period covering at least seven hundred years, from the eighth to the first century B.C.

The endless controversies to which the problem of the origin of the Etruscans or Tyrrhenians has given rise are of mainly theoretical interest. According to the oldest tradition, as recorded by Herodotus, they were emigrants from Asia Minor who came to Italy by sea. Whatever the provenance of the ethnical and cultural elements embodied in the Etruscan people may have been, we find them already established in Italy at the beginning of historic times. Their archaic language, as revealed in documents which still present great difficulties of interpretation, has certainly a basis of words and forms belonging to the primitive linguistic strata of the peoples of Southern Europe and even of Italy; but it is also largely influenced by Indo-European idioms stemming from Eastern Europe, though to a lesser extent than other Italic languages, such as Latin, Umbrian or Oscan.

The prosperity of the Etruscans was probably due to the mineral wealth of their country, still exploited today though only on a relatively small scale (the iron ore in the island of Elba, for instance), but which in early times was remarkably abundant; and also to the fertility of the soil. In conjunction with the development of seaborne commerce and the Phoenician and Greek colonization of the central and western Mediterranean, flourishing urban centers sprang up along the Tyrrhenian coast (Caere, Tarquinii, Vulci, Vetulonia, Populonia) which soon vied with the cities of the Phoenicians and the Greeks in overseas trade and conquests. In this early age of Etruscan history (from the eighth to the sixth century B.C.) the indigenous iron-age culture was tempered by the orientalizing culture introduced by the eastern sea-venturers into all the Mediterranean countries. Thus a highly civilized way of living, strongly imbued with Oriental and Greek elements, developed in the Etruscan cities.

Etruria comprised a league of twelve cities, amongst which were Veii, Chiusi, Perugia, Arezzo and Fiesole, besides those already mentioned. During a certain period the dominion and political control of these powerful communities extended over the greater part of the Italian territory: that is to say Latium (including Rome) and Campania, and on the north the Valley of the Po. But from the sixth century onward the decline of commerce, due no less to international factors than to the aggressive inroads of the Italic peoples from the Apennines and of the Gauls who forced their way across the Alps, led to a rapid collapse of the economic prosperity of the Etruscans, and even of their Empire. The result was that before long Etruria was pressed back behind her frontiers, and soon came under the dominion of Rome (fourth to third centuries), after some desperate attempts at resistance. For some time, however, that is to say until the end of the Republic, the Etruscan cities continued to lead their own autonomous life, with their own institutions, their own art traditions and their own customs. There was even a certain economic and cultural revival, especially in northern Etruria. But during the imperial period the country was completely integrated into the ethnical and cultural unit of Romanized Italy.

The fact that we are fortunate enough to be able to admire Etruscan painting and study it in the originals is due to the nature of the monuments themselves. Save for rare exceptions, they are of a funerary character and consist mainly of sunk tombs dug into the rock, with painted walls.

Quite possibly these decorated hypogea had already been studied in the age of the Renaissance when there was such keen interest in ancient art. We seem to have echoes of this in a poetic description of Corneto (the mediaeval name for Tarquinii) written in the fifteenth century, and in Ariosto's descriptions of enchanted caves (*Orlando Furioso*, III, 15). Michelangelo's drawing of the head of a bearded god wearing a wolf-head must surely have originated from a painted tomb containing the representation of a scene in the underworld. More frequent and extensive discoveries were made in the seventeenth and eighteenth centuries, and above all during the last century, when most of the monuments which we are about to consider were brought to light.

Many of the Etruscan painted tombs known to us from descriptions, sketches, watercolors and the like have been obliterated, or irreparably damaged by time or human agency. At Tarquinii there used to be about sixty tombs and of these only just over twenty have survived. Twenty or so are mentioned at Chiusi, but only three are to be seen today. The partial or total preservation of the paintings is sometimes due to their having been lifted from the walls—a difficult and delicate operation attempted in several cases in the past but without good results, save in the case of a few monuments such as the François Tomb at Vulci, the Bruschi and Tarantola Tombs at Tarquinii, and the Paolozzi Tomb at Chiusi. Recently however the Istituto Centrale del Restauro of Rome has achieved far better results at Tarquinii in the Tombs of the Chariots and of the Triclinium, and at Orvieto in the Golini Tombs, by the use of expert technical procedures.

The painted tombs that still survive are fairly numerous, as can be gathered from the instances given above (at Tarquinii and Chiusi). But obviously they represent only a small fraction of the monuments of this kind that originally existed in the Etruscan cemeteries, since a great many have been destroyed and others are perhaps still waiting to be brought to light. Thus it is evident that the art of sepulchral painting was carried to a quite extraordinary pitch in Etruria, unequaled in any other country of the ancient world before the time of the Roman Empire, with the one exception of Egypt. This must not be taken to mean that the custom of painting the walls of the underground tombs prevailed to the same extent throughout the whole of the Etruscan territory. As in other manifestations of art, local traditions played a large part and had individual characteristics peculiar to each locality. During the primitive stage, when the painting was strongly impregnated with orientalizing elements (from the end of the seventh century B.C. to the beginning of the sixth), painted decoration in the tombs seems to have prevailed throughout the whole of central and southern Etruria, and we also find more or less isolated manifestations of it at Veii, Caere, Cosa, Heba (Magliana) and Chiusi (Clusium). But later, that is to say after the middle of the sixth century, it centered almost exclusively around Tarquinii, and it is there that by far the majority of the existing monuments of the type are to be found. Thus Etruscan tomb painting, especially as regards its archaic period, can be assimilated to the paintings at Tarquinii. This flourishing local tradition persisted, with varying fortunes, but never losing its supremacy, until the late Hellenistic period.

After Tarquinii, Chiusi is the Etruscan city where painted tombs are the most abundant. Here, however, the production seems to be almost entirely confined to the fifth century. Elsewhere the later tomb painting is to be seen only in a few monuments at Orvieto, Vulci and Caere.

Besides wall paintings, we find interesting paintings on other surfaces, notably on terracotta slabs, or *pinakes*, used as facings on tombs or buildings. An important series of these from Caere, dating from the sixth century, has been preserved; also a smaller group belonging to the beginning of the fifth century was found in a sanctuary at Veii. The sarcophagi and urns are as a rule adorned with reliefs, but sometimes with paintings; nearly all the very few examples of this art that have come down to us were found at Tarquinii. Pottery must obviously be excluded from the field of painting properly so called, since in a general way it is confined to a black and red technique which brings out only the drawing. Still we must not overlook the fact that in the decoration of vases attempts were made, now and then, to introduce, by means of polychromy and chiaroscuro, procedures appropriate to painting.

Certainly, if the tomb paintings did not exist, we should know next to nothing of the art world of the Etruscans so far as painting is concerned. In Etruria, as in Greece, sacred, public and private buildings were lavishly decorated both with ornamental reliefs and with paintings. This is proved by the terracotta work embodied in the structure of the temples which, along with decorations (usually polychrome) in relief have subjects painted in the flat. Notable instances of this are the painted slabs of Veii which certainly belonged to the temple, and those of Caere discovered within the precincts of the city. For that matter, there is plenty of information on the subject to be found in ancient writers, particularly in the works of Pliny the Elder (*Natural History*, XXXV, 17 sq. 154). Indeed it was only to be expected that the most significant—whether mural or on slabs—should be the decoration made for buildings in the greater cities. Unfortunately, however, owing to the perishable nature of the material employed and the ravages of time, all these buildings have disappeared, their only remaining vestiges being the terracotta revetment plaques mentioned above. In the underground tombs, on the other hand, protected from the elements, the wonderful decorations have come down to us practically intact. The Etruscans have fared better than the Greeks as regards the preservation of their painting of the pre-Roman period, owing to this very fact that in Etruria it was customary to paint the tombs; whereas the Greeks confined their monumental painting to the decoration of sacred and civil edifices, with the regrettable result that it has almost entirely disappeared.

This circumstance also throws light on the purport of the mural decorations of the Etruscans, the ideology, so to speak, behind them. Like the Italic peoples in general, they seem to have given much attention to the decoration and lay-out of their tombs, and in this resembled their predecessors, the ancient Eastern races, the pre-Hellenic or proto-Hellenic inhabitants of the Aegean and, in historic times, the peoples of Anatolia, Thrace and similar regions. The underlying reason for this practice was the primitive belief that the spirit of the dead man survives in the world beyond the grave—its " eternal home "—and that there it needs protection, sustenance and comfort. At a very early stage the Greeks discarded the magico-religious mentality of the ancient Mediterranean races and adopted other, in a sense more elevated, ideas regarding the destiny of the soul in the after-world. This is why their interest in funerary monuments and rites was less active and less purposeful.

Etruscan tomb painting should not be regarded as merely decorative, nor should it be ascribed merely to family *pietas*, or a vague desire to perpetuate the memory of the dead. It directly concerned the dead man and, anyhow originally, had a precise ritual function of a magico-religious nature; its purpose was to re-create for the dead man his earthly environment, or by means of pictures to prolong the vitalistic power of certain funerary rites.

The choice of subjects was dictated by these considerations. It was only natural that the decorators of the Etruscan tombs were unable to break with the predominating tendencies of archaic art and the precedents of Oriental and Greek models ; hence the fact that, especially in the earliest tomb paintings, we find so many orientalizing themes : *cortèges* of real or fabulous animals, and incidents taken from Greek mythology. These themes must certainly have been frequently utilized for the ornamentation of ordinary houses—which bears out the general view of the tomb as a faithful reproduction of the house of the living man, as to its architecture, decorative adjuncts and furnishing. But alongside representations of an imagined world, there soon began to appear subjects illustrating scenes of everyday life, in which the deceased was thus enabled to take part. Realistic motifs are sometimes found in Greek funerary art, accompanied by a likeness of the dead man, showing him present at a feast ; or else his funeral may be represented. But these are isolated scenes and figure in small compositions on stelae or sepulchral urns; they have no place in the development of large-scale painting or sculpture. In any case the Greek genius tended to idealize and sublimate depictions of this kind, giving them generic rather than specific referents. Etruscan funerary art, on the other hand, dominated as it was by religious exigencies, shows a quite amazing variety of genres and a keen sensitivity, allied with a deliberate preference for the concrete and contemporary, manifested in scenes from everyday life.

It would seem that the ceremonial mourning for the dead, and the rites—bloody or bloodless—and funeral games attending the obsequies had the same mystic, invocatory power as the incidents represented in the paintings. The scenes of banqueting, music-making and festal dancing provided vicarious food and entertainment for the dead and the walls of the tombs are covered with pictures of daily life evoking pleasant hours indoors, in the country or at the seaside. Sometimes these contain no reminder of their association with death, but seem to have been painted to satisfy the artist's taste for that lively, detailed, meticulously accurate rendering of scenes he had observed, which bulked ever larger, as time went on, in the local art tradition. In this respect Etruscan archaic painting of the sixth and fifth centuries B.C. recalls the funerary art of the ancient East and especially that of the Egyptian tombs. In any case its realism strikes a remarkable and suggestive contrast with the mythological themes that figure so predominantly in the repertory of Greek art and indeed stands in a class by itself.

The change in the choice of subjects which makes itself felt from the fourth century onwards was likewise due to considerations of a spiritual order. When the primitive notion that the spirit of the dead man went on living within the tomb lost ground, and was superseded by a belief in a " Land of Shades " corresponding to the Greek Hades, the leading theme of funerary painting became the representation of man's existence in that dim after-life beyond the grave. Thus the realistic approach gave place to visionary concepts of the other world. Yet these imagined scenes of the dead man's future life have neither that special commemorative character nor the mythological allusions we find in some Greek works of art dealing with the same subject—even though the Etruscan painters obviously used these as their models. For the Etruscans still kept to the specific and concrete. The dead whose after-life they depict are definite individuals, the men who were buried in these tombs, and their identity is assured by portraits and inscriptions. They are pictured in the act of taking leave of their loved ones, or on their way to the infernal regions, or else after they have joined the dolorous, awe-inspiring company of the underworld. But even in these gloomy visions of the kingdom of the dead there are frequent realistic touches; for instance in the banqueting scenes which are transported bag and baggage, with all the familiar, customary details of the local scene, into the defunctive setting of Avernus. These scenes of the netherworld are yet another original feature of Etruscan tomb painting, a feature that differentiates it still more from the religious or domestic decorative art, in which predominate mythological subjects of purely Greek inspiration. However, in the wall paintings and notably in the sarcophagi of the fourth century and the Hellenistic period, themes taken from mythology are frequent. As a general rule these relate to battle and bloodshed, and are thus in keeping with that psychological attitude, at once sadistic and morose, which is reflected in the portrayals of the after-life. Perhaps, however, these contain some esoteric, symbolical or religious significance which we are, so far, unable to elucidate.

Having considered Etruscan painting from the viewpoint of its content, we shall now examine the fundamental problem of its artistic value.

These ancient paintings, so remarkable for the boldness of their drawing and the brightness of their color, so ingenuous and yet so elegant, so remote in time and yet so near to our modern sensibility and taste, have an immediate, irresistible appeal, and almost instinctively we are inclined to ascribe to them authentic and positive artistic value. But if we are to give these impressions critical validity we must begin by trying to determine the true historical status of these precious legacies of the past in the light of the general development of art and technical procedures in the ancient world—in short, to ascertain their background.

The first paintings in Etruria that we know of go back, as has been said, to the end of the seventh century or the beginning of the sixth. During this period the art culture of the Mediterranean world was still under the influence of eclectic currents deriving from the achievements of the ancient civilizations of the East. Though the Greek art centers contributed to the elaboration and diffusion of orientalizing trends, yet they were now beginning to impose their own original and powerful stylistic innovations, which were destined completely to transform the Mediterranean art tradition. In any case, the eastern motifs figuring in the modest incunabula of Etruscan painting certainly came by way of Greece, while they also show traces of the influence of primitive Greek, Cretan, Rhodian and Corinthian graphic methods.

In the course of the sixth century Greece took the lead in the art ventures of the Mediterranean peoples. The creative genius and radiant energy of Hellas, together with the great colonizing movements East and West, gave a decided Greek imprint to the phenomenon known as archaic art. It also spread to other races, such as the indigenous peoples of Anatolia in the East and the Etruscans in the West. However, from a stylistic point of view, archaic art is not of a rigorously uniform nature. It shows a copious variety of tendencies, a kaleidoscopic, ever-changing amalgam of tastes, and sometimes even contrasting sensibilities and traditions. This can only be explained as the outcome of a vigorous innovating ferment that spread over a vast geographical area, in countries of widely differing cultural backgrounds.

Indeed the chief characteristic of archaic art culture seems to have been a stimulus to the formation and development of regional currents and local schools. Etruscan archaic art is one of the manifestations of this phenomenon. Neither does it show opposition to Greek art taken as a whole, nor can it simply be dismissed as a weak imitation of Greek models—though each of these views has found modern authorities to endorse it. We are more inclined to say that it tends to re-fashion, within its own ambit, stylistic motifs diffused from various centers of the Greek world; and that it played an active part in the extension of the vast art achievements of the Mediterranean world.

The theory of the actual presence of Greek artists in central Italy is supported by information found in historical sources (e.g. Pliny, *Natural History*, XXXV, 152, 154), and this is borne out by the nature of the monuments themselves. For there are objects of art probably or certainly made on the spot, in Etruria, which are evidently original works and not merely copies of other objects imported from Greece. Moreover, what we know of the economic and cultural conditions of the Etruscan coastal cities in the archaic period justifies the view that they were centers of attraction not only for overseas traffickers who imported Greek products in amazing quantities (to such effect that Greek pottery, for example, is chiefly known from the discoveries made in Etruscan cemeteries), but also for sculptors, potters, painters and metal-workers from different parts of the Hellenic world. We know, too, that even in the archaic period the best artists of the day were often summoned to work in countries far from their native lands. We can picture these foreign masters founding local schools and *botteghe*, and contributing in various ways and in varying degrees to the shaping and development of the taste of the Etruscan artists. In any case an over-all survey of the stylistic currents in Etruria between the end of the seventh century and the beginning of the fifth reveals the interdependence between the themes and forms of the Tyrrhenian region and those of the various centers, remote or near, of Greek artistic production. During the first half of the sixth century, the first Ionic contributions mingle with and superimpose themselves on the influences of the Doric school, whose center was in Corinth. Probably in this stage of art development in the Etruscan cities the Greek colonies of southern Italy and Sicily played a very considerable part. However, towards the middle of the century we find a change taking place that was of vital importance for Etruria. Alongside the Etrurian contacts with Western Greece, we suddenly find close and highly active relations developing with the Greek world of the East, that is to say with the culture and art forms prevailing in the Greek colonies on the west coast of Asia Minor. The influence of the Asiatic centers of Aeolia and Ionia made itself felt preponderantly in Etruscan architecture and painting, the result being a striking affinity between the culture of central Italy and that of regions situated at the far end of the area of Magna Graecia. And it is probable that, specially during this period, artists from Eastern Greece settled in Etruria and that this was connected with the migrations and colonizing movements then in progress from Asia Minor to the Mediterranean West. This East Greek or Ionic art current was dominant in Etruscan production until the end of the sixth century, when new tendencies stemming from the great art centers of Greece itself (and especially from Athens) brought about a change of taste—a change that characterized the last phase of archaism.

Although falling in line with the general development of archaic art, Etruria, as we have said, does not seem to have accepted the teachings of the Greek masters passively; features distinctively Etruscan, as compared with the *ensemble* of archaic cultures, hold their own. In these we see the survival of ancient local traditions of Oriental or paleo-Hellenic, if not actually prehistoric, origin (as evidenced in the special nature of the Etruscan monuments and painting), a mingling and overlapping of various foreign contributions, the generally conservative tendencies of the indigenous schools, and finally brilliant innovations by certain individual artists. Among these artists was that great genius known as the Master of the Apollo of Veii, who has rightly or wrongly been identified as Vulca of Veii, the one artist of ancient Italy to figure by name in the literary tradition. Thus in the productions of archaic art it is relatively easy to identify and distinguish between what was made in Etruria and what was made for instance in Sicily, Athens, or the Cyclades.

The output of the Etruscan artists assumes particular importance during the second half of the sixth century, and during the phase of belated archaism—known as the " severe style "—which predominated in Etruria during the first half of the fifth century. And it is the paintings which have most to tell us about these two periods of great artistic activity, during which the works of the Etruscans ranked in the forefront of all the art production of the Mediterranean world. These paintings must be regarded as spontaneous, original expressions of the aspirations and talents of those who made them, and this despite the traces inevitably present in them of schemas or formulas of an international kind, and even though the cultural level and genius of the artists vary considerably from monument to monument. The decoration of a tomb was not regarded as a humble task of little moment that could be assigned to any ordinary craftsman. Given the sacred nature of the paintings and the loving care lavished by the Etruscans on the decoration and equipment of the abodes of their dead, and when we take into account the standing of such families as could afford the luxury of these private monuments, it is obvious that as a rule only the ablest and most admired artists in the Etruscan cities were given commissions for the painting of the tombs.

As regards the archaic painting of the great Ionico-Etruscan period and the " severe style," we are fully justified in appraising these pictures on their own merits as works of art, and discounting any theory that they may be copies or reflections of outstanding originals which have been lost. For none who have seen these paintings *in situ* but have had an absolute conviction of being in the presence of works of genuinely high quality, and not merely the productions of journeymen.

The great diversity of inspiration and characteristics to be found in tomb paintings of the same city, and of approximately the same period, goes both to prove the originality of the artists concerned and the creative freedom with which they approached their tasks. Thus we have every incentive for finding out something about their personalities and methods of expression. As regards these painters some modern scholars have advanced the hypothesis that in certain cases the tombs of Tarquinii must have been decorated by the Greek artists whose presence and activity in the Etruscan territory is well established. Indeed it seems natural that, since the best artists available were enlisted for the painting of the tombs, recourse should have been had whenever practicable to the foreign leaders of schools, who presumably were exercising a very strong influence on local taste. However, it must be remembered that in a cultural group such as that of the Etruscans during the last decades of the sixth century and the beginning of the fifth, it can be no easy matter distinguishing between the influence of presumed Greek masters and that of the best of their Etruscan followers and emulators, merely on the strength of the stylistic characteristics of the works of art in question. Nor can we accept any *a priori* theory—dubious at best and far too sweeping—that the most refined works are necessarily by Greeks and the poorer ones by Etruscans. What really matters is the artistic conceptions of these painters and their aspirations, whether they worked as masters or pupils and whatever their country of origin. All the more so because in any case even the Greek artists adapted their genius and their execution to concepts stemming from the beliefs and customs of the Etruscan community and implicit in the very nature of their tomb paintings. Therefore it may be said that so far as archaic painting in Etruria is concerned, art historians need not occupy themselves with the problem— abstract and insoluble at best—of the nationality of the artists, and we should do better to try to elucidate the personalities of these painters, their artistic formation, their predilections and their qualities, taking as the starting-point of our researches the evidence of the surviving monuments.

But the problem changes considerably, almost we might say radically, when we move on from the archaic phase to the period of Classical and Hellenistic influences. The consequences of the political and economic events which were taking place in the Mediterranean at the beginning of the fifth century were of far greater cultural importance than is generally supposed. The Greek world, threatened on the East by the Persian Empire and on the West by the might of Carthage, tended to become self-contained and engrossed in building up its own national civilization, whose artistic aspect is mirrored by the classical age. The genius of such painters as Polygnotos, Micon, Zeuxis, Parrhasios, and of sculptors such as Myron, Pheidias and Polyklitos constituted landmarks in the history of human cultural progress. But the great innovating activities of these pioneers seem to have been almost entirely confined to some important centers of Greece proper, at Athens and in the Peloponnesus. The peripheric and colonial schools which had so greatly prospered in the archaic period declined, disappeared or came under the control of the mother-cities. Even the international character of archaic art lost its *raison d'être* with the diminution or breakdown of the political, economic and cultural relations which had united the Hellenic communities with the Asiatic lands and with the western Mediterranean. Thus Etruria became isolated and underwent a serious economic crisis; which meant it was no longer able to maintain the position it had had in the sixth century as a thriving trading center, and a much favored market for Greek merchandise and works of art.

This is the reason why, in the art traditions of Etruria, the conceptions and methods of archaic art lingered on well into the fifth century—as is evident when we examine the Etruscan painting of the period. Losing contact more and more with the Hellenic world, it went on repeating, within a sphere that now was strictly local, the motifs of the severe style which had made good in the early years of the century. Only here and there do we find reflections of the contemporary developments of Greek graphic art. Meanwhile inspiration tended steadily to dry up, and fewer monuments were erected, for reasons which had nothing to do with art but were mainly of an economic nature.

Thus with the gradual disappearance of archaic and sub-archaic traditions, and the equally gradual assimilation of the new methods of classical Hellenic art by the Etruscan schools, Etruscan art, from the end of the fifth century onwards, presents entirely new problems to the art historian. The basic question—that of the relations between Greek art and Etruria and the originality, or subordination, of the latter as regards the former—must be envisaged on lines quite other than those appropriate to its archaic phase. After the cessation of the age-old interdependence of the Mediterranean peoples and the " family likeness " of their ways of living, the Etruscans were led by the force of circumstances (or by differences of temperament) to estrange themselves completely from the evolution of classical art, and even lost to some extent the capacity of understanding and assimilating the notions that lay behind its spiritual equilibrium and feeling for harmonious form. None the less, the strong, never-failing fascination exercised by Hellenic civilization incited the Etruscan painters to align themselves with the taste of the age and to imitate classical models, by way of objects directly imported from Greece or contacts with the Hellenic or Hellenized centers of southern Italy. But this assimilation went no farther than a more or less faithful copying of certain well-known compositions, used as models in many parts of the Mediterranean world. They also tried to adapt these motifs to their own composition by procedures which, at best, were limited to a superficial reproduction of the lay-out of the Greek originals but showed a total incomprehension of their spirit. In any case, by a reversal of the process obtaining in the archaic period, Greek art now penetrated Etruria as a foreign art, and the richer it was in suggestions, the more servilely was it imitated. It is in this sense that we can speak of the " provincialism " of Etruscan art and its dependence upon Greek art; and it is this that justifies us in seeing the mark of Etruscan craftsmanship in works that are treated in a decadent or clumsy style. But our appraisals of the work turned out by Etruscan artists during the fourth century and in the Hellenistic period should not be limited to considerations of the imitative elements—of lesser importance, in the last analysis—we detect in them. We should, rather, fix our attention on that other world of very different emotions, aspirations and achievements they reveal to us. The heritage of ancient traditions and racial predispositions, a tenacious loyalty to thoroughly assimilated archaic themes, the reactions following the clash of old and new artistic tendencies, spiritual exigencies deriving from the religious and social mentality of the Etruscans—all alike contributed to form the background of the new and striking developments in Etruscan art. We are fully justified in believing that during this period there were pioneer artists of indisputable genius in Etruria, whose inspiration and tendencies towards an art of fantasy were almost entirely independent of the Hellenic spirit. Above all, the pictures show a great feeling for direct, spontaneous, concrete expression, achieved by the dissociation of the linear and plastic forms of classic art and by a deliberate stressing of individual elements—characteristics which are particularly in evidence in these artists' treatment of portraits. Indeed it is in the portrait that we see the high originality of Etruscan art, whether viewed in isolation or as forming a part, and an important part, of the vaster art movement which then was taking form, and which is known as Italo-Roman.

When studying the paintings we cannot fail to be struck by the number and variety of the cross-currents pervading the world of Etruscan art between the fourth and first century B.C. Here the diversity of themes is paralleled by an equal diversity of artistic cultural levels, a state of things quite unknown in the archaic period. As for the mythological compositions obviously copied from Greek models, we must go warily in forming an opinion regarding them, owing to the secondary and imitative character of the works of art that have come down to us. Thus the critic has to take account of two factors, and determine both the artistic value of the originals and the qualities, whether positive or negative, of their Etruscan interpretations. The problem becomes still more intricate in the case of compositions in which indigenous creative genius seems to take over elements properly belonging to the Greek repertory and to adapt them to its own requirements, or to invent type-formulas enabling the portrayal of real or imaginary personages of its own world. Here we must be careful to distinguish between the negative process of reducing and attenuating the original forms, and the positive manifestations of new stylistic experiments. Particularly interesting are the artists' appreciation of idiosyncrasies of appearance and the expressive values in their portraits.

The technique of Etruscan painting offers an interesting field of discovery for the researcher. The partial investigations which have so far been made leave much ground still unexplored; still they have sufficed to prove that the artists' procedures varied according to the period, and also according to the nature of the surface to be painted. However, it would seem that these procedures can be reduced to certain generalized methods of work, applicable to the greater part of the ancient painting that has come down to us.

The preparation is of considerable importance. Obviously the simplest method was that of applying the colors directly on to the surface to be decorated. In the tombs this was the hewn rock, usually tufaceous, which however was carefully smoothed and polished—though not enough to prevent the decorated surface from remaining somewhat irregular and granulated. Owing to its natural moisture the rock face tended to absorb the colors and they accordingly were mixed into a more or less binding medium. This was the method usually followed in the very ancient tombs, in the tombs of Chiusi and also in some of the archaic tombs of Tarquinii, among them the Tomb of the Baron (though here, as a matter of fact, a greyish undercoat is perceptible beneath the linework and colors of each figure). Also in the painted terracotta slabs we find occasional instances of this direct application of the colors; a procedure regularly followed in the decoration of the stone sarcophagi.

Most frequently, however, the painting was made on a foundation of plaster—extremely thin in the case of the terracotta slabs and the earliest wall paintings. In the later tombs, however, this foundation may be over two centimeters thick. The slabs of Caere and Veii have a very thin coat or, rather, they are covered with what is known to potters as a 'slip' made of clay and lime, of an ivory or greyish color tending towards yellow. In the archaic tombs of Tarquinii we usually find an equally thin layer of clay, the surface of which is finely coated with limewash. Strands of peat are present in the texture of the plaster in the Tomb of the Chariots (recalling methods employed in eastern wall paintings); this use of vegetable tissue for the purpose of reinforcing the coat of plaster was actually a technical process better suited to large-scale painting in edifices above ground than to that in the damp underground sepulchral chambers.

Often the application of the color seems to have been preceded by a preparatory drawing, incised in the wall surface, sometimes confined to straight lines framing the scenes and figure groups, but sometimes also tracing the outlines and even details of the subjects represented. Particularly interesting and revealing are the traces of *pentimenti*, passages in which the artist has changed his mind, and the final drawing, while following the general lines of the incised sketch, slightly diverges from them. These *pentimenti* obviously rule out, in certain cases, any theory of the employment of mechanical methods of reproduction on the craftsmen's part. Also, they confirm the hypothesis of a certain amount of inventive spontaneity on the part of the decorator.

Thus, in archaic wall painting, both the incising and the application of the color were carried out while the plaster was still wet, which involves immediate execution, or anyhow one enabling all the successive stages of the painting to be carried out within a relatively short space of time. In the tombs the natural moisture of the walls probably facilitated the painters' task; there was little risk of the plaster's drying too rapidly. The use of the true fresco technique in the Etruscan tombs has now been definitely proved. But no final decision has yet been arrived at regarding the possibility that in some later tombs tempera colors were applied on the plaster surface after it had dried— as was often done in murals of the Roman period.

The pigments used were either mineral or vegetable, and such information as we have about their composition confirms what is already known about ancient painting in general. For instance, the use of white made from chalk, reds from oxide of iron, blue from lapis lazuli and black from charcoal has been established. The quality and variety of the pigments must certainly have been conditioned by the general development of art, or by the special technical and stylistic trends of each period. Usually, however, the richness of the color scale seems to be in direct relation with the quality and delicacy of the painting itself. In the oldest monuments, and later too, in less important works, only black, white and red are used, with yellow sometimes added : that is to say the traditional classical colors of Greek painting. In addition to these, blues and greens make their appearance in the Ionico-Etruscan phase; by mixing or diluting these colors, a varied scale of half tones was obtained, comprising ivory whites, pinks, browns, mauves, greys and so on. It should be borne in mind that what has come down to us of Greek painting and polychrome sculpture points to the use in Greece of other colors besides the four traditional ones. But it is only in Etruria that we see a great variety of half tones employed by the painters; this is particularly true of the archaic period, since from the fourth century onwards their palette became more restricted. Drawing plays the chief part in the construction of the figures; contours are defined by a more or less continuous line and the open spaces thus delimited are filled in with color. This practice is rigorously observed in the oldest paintings; but actually it lies at the base of all archaic painting. Until the fifth century it is accompanied in Etruria by an over-all, uniform coloring of each of the areas of the inner surface, so that the chromatic effect, sometimes quite remarkable, is achieved chiefly by juxtaposition and contrasts of these colored areas. However, this does not exclude (anyhow in certain cases and in monuments of particularly mature style and technique) the presence of details marked by patches of blended color, or even of gradations from one colored surface to another. The technical achievements of classical and Hellenistic painting, that is to say shading, *sfumato* and the abandoning of clean-cut outlines, are reflected in the Etruscan painted monuments of the fourth century and the Hellenistic age. The successful use of graduated color is a noteworthy feature of some of the outstanding works of these new times; but there are plenty of signs in Etruria of the diffusion, from Hellenistic centers, of still more highly evolved procedures, such as the treatment of light in patches of color, which culminated in the Hellenistic-Roman painting of the early Empire.

But the conservatism, not to say conventionality of the Etruscan schools, especially in the last phase, is not to be denied. Thus the old traditions of figure drawing, based wholly upon outline, also make their presence felt insistently alongside the new techniques, not only in the less important monuments (where this might be attributed to the naïvety of craftsmen who knew no better) but also in some carefully executed paintings of high artistic value.

What we have set forth above regarding the content, formal development and technique of Etruscan painting may, it is hoped, be of assistance in enabling the reader to understand and to appraise the artistic genius and the mentality of this remarkable people, which, allowing for the limitations of period and place, achieved so high a standard of production. But, as we have already suggested, the pictorial achievement of ancient Etruria, viewed from another angle, can claim a still more important place in the history of world art, when we remember that it is almost the only art to give a concrete illustration of the general evolution of ancient painting in the Graeco-Italic world during several centuries of the first millennium B.C.

Whereas, for Italy, we have a copious and varied stock of material to go on— not to mention the innumerable examples of Italo-Roman decorative art that have come down to us—, it is quite otherwise with Greek painting. The number and value of direct illustrations of Greek painting (if we disregard the vase paintings) are quite insignificant. This is why a tendency has prevailed to assume that Italy was the home of painting and color whereas Greece was that of form and sculpture.

Actually, this idea, like many conventional ideas, is wholly erroneous. The writers of the classical past extolled enthusiastically and unanimously the art of the great Greek painters, especially those of the classical period (from Polygnotos of Thasos to Apelles), but also those of the archaic and Hellenistic periods. Surely, when we read their glowing encomia, we can but be convinced that their achievements were not merely on a par with, but even superior to those of the world-famous sculptors, and manifested no less brilliantly the genius of Hellas. Unhappily this world of Greek paintings, with all its wonders, is lost for ever; this is due to the wanton dispersal and destruction of the pictures and, in the case of the wall paintings, to the ruined state of the edifices that housed them. Nothing remains of them but a few contemporary reflections in the painted vases, and some dubious echoes in Hellenistico-Roman decorative painting and in minor forms of art: ornaments in relief, graving on metal and the like.

In view of this widespread destruction the Etruscan paintings, regional or provincial as their characteristics may be and though they have a style and content peculiar to themselves, have inestimable value as collateral and contemporary sources of information. True, they do not enable us to see what Greek painting was at its splendid best, but they give us a fair idea of it, especially as regards technical procedures, certain formal effects and certain aspects of its historical development, regarding which the indirect and minor sources of information mentioned above are inadequate.

Viewed from this angle, Etruscan painting may be looked upon as a kind of connecting link—of high documentary value—between the pictorial art of the Greeks (with which, as we have seen, it was so closely associated in various ways) and that of the Romans. The latter constitutes a direct continuation of Hellenistic painting, especially on Italian soil, though also in its provincial ramifications, despite the fact that its evolution follows a rhythm of its own and that it displays an innate capacity for innovation sponsoring a very real and fruitful originality in the field of creative art. However, Italian painting of the late Republic and of the Empire was bound to absorb and retain certain elements inherited from the early indigenous pictorial traditions, and amongst these the Etruscan tradition seems by far the most important, in view of the influence it appears to have exercised on the pictorial art of other Italic races, as is indicated by the decoration of the tombs discovered in Campania and Apulia. Furthermore, this tradition of Etruscan painting, which persisted in the immediate vicinity of Rome until the end of the last century of the Republic, was, as we have seen, deeply imbued with Hellenistic influences. Thus the transition from one pictorial cycle to the other presents itself rather as a phase of a continuous evolutionary process than as a definite break with the past.

Indeed all that we learn from the monuments themselves confirms the existence of these presumed links. In the last tomb paintings of the Etruscans, decorative elements, technical procedures and stylistic trends directly recalling the contemporary wall paintings of Rome and Pompeii in the initial phases of the so-called first and second styles make their appearance. An even more important point is that some of the characteristics peculiar to Etruscan painting in the Hellenistic period can be seen, more or less clearly, in the most spontaneous and sincere productions of the Roman painters: an effort to render expression in portraits, a tendency to break up organic form in the accentuation of specific details or in conveying a mass effect (a crowd for instance), and the bold combination of a color technique all in shade effects and nuances with a developed linear system. Some of these procedures seem to derive from those popular art currents which, after the gradual weakening of Hellenistic inspiration, re-emerged during the last centuries of the Empire. Indeed some aspects of Etruscan painting seem even to anticipate, and often in a striking manner, the motifs and methods characteristic of Late Antiquity.

These are amongst the considerations justifying our claim that Etruscan painting should be regarded—and not merely from the chronological angle—as the first chapter of the history of Italian painting.

1

THE PRIMITIVES

FROM ORIENTAL INFLUENCES TO THE IONICO-ETRUSCAN PHASE

(SIXTH CENTURY B.C.)

Unfortunately the only surviving tokens of the earliest phase of Etruscan painting are a few much damaged tomb frescos: those of the Campana Tomb at Veii and the Tombs of the Painted Lions and the Painted Animals at Caere. As for the other monuments of the kind, only their memory remains. They contained pictures of real or fabulous animals, sometimes of human figures and stylized plant designs. These motifs were taken from the orientalizing style of decoration, which was imported into Etruria during the seventh century from the centers of Syria, Cyprus and the Aegean, along with precious objects made of gold, silver and ivory, painted vases (chiefly of Rhodian and Corinthian manufacture) and probably textiles and carpets. This style became very popular in Etruria. The drawing in these decorations is abstract, the color intense and unrealistic. The Veii paintings, with their spindle-legged horses, suggest Cretan influences.

This kind of decoration prevailed between the close of the seventh century and the beginning of the sixth, and was then replaced by more elaborate compositions in which the human figure played a considerable part. The first painted terracotta slabs from Caere belong to an intermediary stage between these two decorative styles. From the stylistic point of view, Doric influence had made good and the first Ionic influences were now beginning to appear.

However, archaic painting in Etruria had not fully established itself as a cultural and artistic phenomenon, and did not attain definite expressive power, until the second half of the sixth century. During this period the whole Mediterranean West seems to have been traversed by art currents issuing from the flourishing centers of eastern Greece, that is to say from the Aeolian and Ionic cities on the Asia Minor coast and from the near-by Aegean islands. This is more likely to have been the result of historical events which led navigators, farmers and East Greek refugees to migrate and settle in the West, both inland and on the seaboard, than to have been due to normal trade relations. Particularly important was the colonization of the coast of Mediterranean France, Corsica and Southern Italy by the Phocaeans; their political antagonism with Etruria, by whom they had been defeated in the naval battle of Alalia (ca. 540 B.C.), did not necessarily rule out active cultural intercourse.

It is highly probable that the chief place of ingress and diffusion for the currents of East Greek art in Etruria was the city of Caere, which had played a leading part in the battle of Alalia and was at this time a rich, populous metropolis, with an active foreign trade. Abundant evidence of this is furnished by the painted vases of East Greek style, as regards some of which (the so-called " Caeretan hydriai " for instance) there can be little doubt that they were manufactured on the spot by immigrant Ionic artists. Also the painted fictile slabs of the period have characteristics closely resembling those of the vases.

However, we have good reason for believing that large-scale wall painting flourished above all at Tarquinii, where East Greek forms were easily adjusted to the requirements of an art whose inspiration derived from Etruscan religious beliefs and customs. The representation of reality completely replaced mythological subjects. It may be said that, irrespective of the origin and nationality of the individual artists, the paintings of Tarquinii in this period stand for a very definite achievement and one of high artistic significance within the framework of archaic art. This may suitably be designated the " Ionico-Etruscan " phase. As a local phenomenon it lasted until the early years of the fifth century, when the art of Eastern Greece had long since lost its appeal for the Etruscans.

THE BOCCANERA SLABS

Painting on terracotta slabs was widely diffused in the archaic world, no less than mural painting. The slabs found at Caere are classed among the "whitened slabs," πίνακες λελευκωμένοι, whose invention is traditionally attributed to the ancient Greek painter Kraton of Sicyonia. After being smoothed, the surface is covered with a light undercoat on which the figures are first traced in graffito and then painted.

The form of these slabs is of a special kind and never varies. They form oblong rectangles and as used in decoration are placed vertically lengthwise. The lower part has a kind of dado patterned with parallel vertical stripes or occasionally checkered. Above this comes the picture proper. This did not usually end at the edge of the slab but joined up right and left with other elements. In many cases these slabs were made to form part of quite large compositions. The top contained ornamental motifs (braids or wavy lines), or in some cases a tiny pictorial frieze, or a projecting cornice. Thus when placed side by side these slabs formed a continuous frieze. They were almost certainly intended to be used as revetments for the inner walls of rooms, and in fact produced much the same effect as actual frescos.

The fact that some of the Caeretan slabs (for instance a fragment now in the Berlin Museum and those recently discovered and now to be seen in the Museum of Villa Giulia, Rome) were not brought to light in the necropolis but within the city area, is particularly significant. For it shows that they were used for the decoration of public and of sacred edifices, and perhaps of private houses, as well as for tombs. Thus they count among the extremely rare survivals of other than funerary Etruscan painting. In this connection we may note that Pliny explicitly mentions the existence of paintings done in a strongly archaic style in the edifices of Caere.

The examples of this very special class of painting that have come down to us are numerous and, though all belong to the sixth century, considerably varied. The oldest group is represented by the five Boccanera slabs, named after their discoverer; they came from a tomb and are now in London at the British Museum. Another group of five slabs and a sixth of a somewhat different type, known as the Campana slabs, were likewise found in the necropolis and are now in Paris at the Louvre. There are also the above-mentioned Berlin fragment and a series of fragments discovered during recent excavations at Caere; these are of various types but rather similar in style to the Campana group.

All the Boccanera slabs are of the same size and have the same characteristics; there can be no doubt that they formed part of the same decorative *ensemble*. Two of them have pictures of crouching sphinxes facing in opposite directions (perhaps originally placed opposite each other on either side of a door); the other three are sections of a continuous frieze. One of the other slabs depicts a man in the vestments of an Etruscan priest in the act of welcoming another man carrying a scepter or a military emblem. Behind the latter is a woman with a lance and a crown. Three women figure on each of the other two slabs.

The subject of this picture is of quite exceptional interest and significance since it furnishes an example of the orientalizing repertory of the more ancient tombs. This fabulous monster is elegantly drawn on the rectangular ground, resting on its hind paws and its left front paw, and raising the other. Its tail is curled round one of its legs. Its large wings of multicolored feathers fan out upwards in volutes. The geometric construction of the body and of the head, with its rigid profile forming a straight line from the forehead to the pointed nose, and its large wide-open eye placed frontally, exhibit a strongly marked archaism. The colors— white, black, reddish and dark brown filling clearly demarcated planes—are applied in a schematic, fantastic manner: in patches on the body and alternately in the feathers of the wings. The fascination of this figure lies in the slender limbs and in the decorative effect of the gay coloring.

The fact that the Boccanera slabs belong to the decoration of a tomb is not sufficient to justify the interpretation of the frieze as a funerary scene, although a woman on one of the slabs is holding out a branch of what looks like pomegranate, a plant sacred to the infernal divinities, and another seems to be entwined by a serpent. The

26

repertory of the most ancient Etruscan tomb paintings has a great variety of fantastic and mythological subjects, as is evidenced by the decoration of the orientalizing tombs of Caere and Veii and can also be seen in the Tomb of the Bulls at Tarquinii. Though the figures of the Boccanera slabs have details which realistically illustrate Etruscan costumes and accessories, such as the attributes of the priest, it is not possible to assign this intriguing scene to the category of subjects taken from real life, characterized by the repertory of the wall paintings of the archaic Etruscan tombs: that is to say, funerals with banquets, music, dancing and athletic contests. There remains a possibility of its being a mythological subject, though embodying locally inspired motifs and allusions.

THREE FEMALE FIGURES. SLAB FROM CAERE. BRITISH MUSEUM, LONDON.

The inclusion of elements depicting indigenous costumes has nevertheless considerable bearing on the history of these paintings, from the angle of their historico-artistic genealogy. The construction of the figures, the profile faces, the conventionalization of the drapery, the relationship between design and color, clearly show the influence of Corinthian black-figured pottery. Yet neither the influence of Corinthian drawing and even less that of contemporary Attic drawing can fully account for the characteristics of these paintings, and especially the human figures, with their massive bodies, round faces, exaggeratedly sharp profiles and elongated eyes; this is especially true as regards the way the general structure and the details are delineated by flowing, sinuous lines. This type of stylization probably indicates the effect of other influences as well—which can easily be identified as East Greek and Ionic, also by reason of the transparency of the drapery and some incidental details such as the peaked shoes. The importation of Ionic motifs into Etruria before the first half of the sixth century is also apparent in contemporary sculpture ; as a matter of fact similar developments have been traced in the Greek artistic production of Southern Italy, especially after the discovery of the great frieze with carved metopes of the " treasury " of the sanctuary of Hera at the mouth of the Sele. And indeed it is reasonable to assume that the earliest Ionic influences penetrated into Etruria through contacts with the centers of Magna Graecia.

Nevertheless, irrespective of stylistic inspirations from the Greek world, the Boccanera slabs are obviously an indigenous product, and in fact we find in them a spontaneous, " popular " atmosphere. This is due not only to the presence of iconographic details relating to Etruscan costumes. There is a primitive, sketchy, somewhat awkward treatment of the figures, compensated for by a vivacity of attitude and gesture and a certain amount of facial expression. All the cultural influences mentioned above are fused together in this unpretentious, facile and discursive art. The making of these paintings may be attributed to the second quarter, or rather towards the middle of the sixth century B.C.

HORSE'S HEAD. DETAIL FROM ACHILLES IN AMBUSH.
TOMB OF THE BULLS, TARQUINII.

TOMB OF THE BULLS

The paintings in the Tomb of the Bulls are amongst the most ancient of the extant decorations at Tarquinii; they probably date from a little after the middle of the sixth century. The painted surfaces were confined to the triangular pediments and to the back wall of the first chamber. Here we find a painted frieze along the wall, with rather curious subjects: two bulls, one of them with a human head, and two erotic groups. Between the doors is a large mythological picture of Greek inspiration, to which is added a motif of little trees hung with fillets. The subject-matter of these pictures is composite and varied, most of the elements being of a fantastic order. One gets an impression that the painters of Tarquinii were feeling their way towards the formulas which were afterwards employed to such wonderful effect.

The young Trojan prince Troilus comes to water his horses at the fountain. He is naked except for pointed shoes and an armlet. His tawny hair streams out behind him and he is carrying a long staff in his left hand. He is loosely seated on a mettlesome horse with long legs, a small, restless head and a bristling grey mane. A wooded landscape is suggested by the branches and plants filling the empty space around the lonely horseman. A dwarf palmtree, rising in the center of the picture, in front of the rider, almost hides the fountain, which also is surrounded by bushes denser and straighter than the others. The fountain itself is a decorated polychrome structure, built of squared stone blocks; it has a base and cornices, and two lions on the top. From the mouth of the lion on the right water is spouting into a basin beneath. This little scene enacted in the vast peace of the silent wood has the glamour of an old-world fairy-tale. But it is a treacherous glamour; from behind the fountain where he has been lying in ambush there suddenly leaps forth a warrior, wearing a red loin-cloth, a Corinthian helmet and greaves about his legs. His right arm is raised to strike. It is Achilles, incarnation of warlike blood-lust, about to slay the son of Priam.

This incident from the Trojan cycle figures in archaic Greek sculpture and pottery and we find the general lay-out of the composition repeated, with very slight variations, in all these depictions, whatever their provenance may be. This goes to show that all derive from an ancient model that, like so many proto-Hellenic creations of the kind, was diffused throughout the vast geographical area of the archaic world. But it is only here at Tarquinii that we find it figuring as a full-size picture. We might even go so far as to say that this picture in the Tomb of the Bulls is the only complete, fully integrated example that has come down to us of archaic mythological painting, properly so called, and that its documentary value is unique, not only as regards Etruscan, but also as regards Hellenic art.

Quite possibly the artist worked from a model actually before his eyes or else was repeating a theme which he had dealt with before, making use of type patterns for the individual figures. Nevertheless the hesitations we perceive in the incised outlines and even in the lines of the painting itself (this is especially evident in the horse) show that he was drawing and painting free-hand, not copying mechanically, and was giving rein, within limits, to his own inventive genius.

That the stylistic inspiration of the picture is fundamentally Ionic—or, more precisely, Ionico-Asiatic—is proved by the soft plumpness of the figures, and by details of the shape of Troilus's slanting face: the receding forehead, long neck and wind-blown hair. But traces of other influences are no less apparent. Particularly curious are certain elements testifying to an entirely different source of inspiration: the drawing of the Doric painted vases of Sparta; notably the typical pomegranate pattern of the decorative band above the picture and the sober, precise and simplified handling of animals. Obviously the painter of the Tomb of the Bulls had a composite artistic formation; perhaps he had originally been trained in a Dorian school, and then became familiarized with the Ionic models and procedures in vogue throughout Etruria. But the presence of naturalistic details which were subsequently to play so large a part in the paintings

ACHILLES IN AMBUSH. TOMB OF THE BULLS, TARQUINII.

of Tarquinii (for instance the sharply drawn plant motifs studding the empty spaces and tending to suggest a landscape) prove that this artist, even if not to be regarded as an inspired innovator, was a skillful exponent of the culture and techniques of his time.

Here we have a bizarre detail of the frieze that runs over the doors and the scene of *Achilles in Ambush*. The bull has a fantastically long tail and its head, with the strange sky-blue protruding eyes set on different levels, is slewed round so that the massive sweep of the horns is seen front-view. It adheres to the lower edge of the frieze, overlapping in places the pomegranate border; one might almost think it has retreated to the left-hand corner of the white expanse, disturbed by the presence of the near-by erotic group. Whereas its monstrous, human-headed counterpart on the opposite side has already lowered its horns and seems about to charge another loving couple.

This primitive composition owes its effectiveness to the harsh, irregular drawing. Except for the traditional treatment of the hind quarters, the bull gives the impression of having been sketched in rapidly, spontaneously, in a sudden gust of inspiration. The fantastic coloring adds to the queer fascination of this picture; the muzzle and body are pink, the shoulders red-brown, while the hair on the animal's belly and breast, its horns and hoofs are blue.

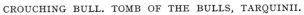

CROUCHING BULL. TOMB OF THE BULLS, TARQUINII.

THE CAMPANA SLABS

The set of painted terracotta slabs from Caere, now in the Louvre and generally known under the name of " the Campana slabs," may be ascribed to the same class as the Boccanera slabs and perhaps stems from the same traditional school of craftsmanship. However there are some points of difference and in any case the Campana slabs are probably of a little later date.

Five of them seem to come from the same frieze, which, however, it is difficult to re-assemble and interpret. Three slabs have sloping cuts in their upper part which form as it were a projecting cornice, and another has been cut through vertically, with the result that one of the figures is sliced from top to bottom. Thus it would seem that these slabs were not originally made for the tomb in which they were found. In view of the fact that similar fragments have been found in other parts of the city, the theory that these slabs once formed part of some public or private building has much to commend it. The following are the themes portrayed :

(1) Two bearded, elderly men are seated on folding chairs facing each other; they are wearing Greek tunics, mantles and peaked shoes. One of them holds a scepter, the other is resting his head on his hand in an attitude of pensive sadness. Above them, on the right, a winged female figure is shooting arrows towards them.

(2) A winged youth wearing a short jacket and carrying a woman in his arms is stepping forward briskly, along with another man who is bearded, wears a similar costume and is carrying a bow and arrow.

(3) A naked youth, his eyes turned to his right, is lifting his right hand to his mouth, while with his left he touches an altar built of blocks of various colors and with a molded plinth. The sacrificial fire is burning on the altar, while a pillar with a curved echinus does duty symbolically for the temple.

(4) Three persons are advancing from left to right; one, a bearded man, wearing a cloak, carries a bow and arrows; a woman wearing a chiton, vest and mantle, holds a branch in her right hand. The third, a man, carries a lance.

(5) Owing to the broken state of the slab, only two of the three figures coming from the right remain: a woman and a young man wearing a mantle over his jacket.

These scenes are usually regarded as illustrating a funeral rite, but this theory has little to support it; given the variety of the figures (some obviously supernatural) and the complex nature of the acts that are taking place, the subject is almost certainly of a mythological order. But it is impossible to determine precisely what myth is being enacted; of various suggestions, the least improbable seems that we have here the Sacrifice of Iphigenia.

A sixth slab, found in the same place, belongs to another frieze, as is evident from the difference in the decoration and the style. It shows a figure with a scepter seated in front of an effigy of a goddess, with a snake gliding past beneath. The subject here (probably also mythological) is equally indeterminate.

It is commonly thought—but almost certainly mistakenly—that this scene shows a dead woman being carried away by a 'genius' of death. But any conception of this sort seems foreign to archaic Etruscan art; and it may be we have here a picture of Iphigenia being carried to the sacrificial altar, in which case the man carrying a bow and arrows would probably be Apollo. The composition, with its finely balanced horizontals and diagonals, implements a skillfully conceived geometrical design—the figures are strongly built and sturdy—and as in the Boccanera slabs, contours are defined by clean-cut, regular lines and the colors applied in flat, even tones.

The same characteristics can be seen in the picture representing two seated men (see page opposite), in which the presence of some modern restorations can be detected. The special atmosphere emanating from these figures is due to the rigidly controlled, architectural structure and the static equilibrium of the composition. This is especially noticeable in the geometric treatment of the elongated hands and fingers and the broad, tranquil rhythm of the vast painted surfaces. Nevertheless the artist's use of smoothly flowing curves gives an impression profoundly different from that produced by any contemporary Attic or Corinthian drawing, in which dry, straight lines prevail. Thus we have here unmistakable evidence of an East Greek inspiration.

WOMAN CARRIED OFF BY A WINGED BEING. SLAB FROM CAERE. LOUVRE, PARIS.

In the present state of our knowledge the problem of archaic painting at Caere involves many difficulties. There is no question that archaic painting enjoyed a considerable vogue in this town about the middle of the sixth century B.C., as is proved by mentions of it made in ancient literature. Apart from the traces of decorations in the early orientalizing tombs (Painted Lions, Painted Animals), our most direct information on the subject is supplied by the painted slabs or plaques. However, we cannot leave wholly out of account the historiated earthenware in the Graeco-Oriental style that has been discovered and which (some of it anyhow) was presumably manufactured at Caere; particularly the group of Caeretan *hydriai*.

The oldest type of slabs, the Boccanera, shows various influences, some Corinthian, some Ionic. None the less it is of an essentially local, unambitious order and naïve, if full of vigor. Whilst the five Campana slabs representing sacrificial scenes are affiliated to the Boccanera slabs by their technique and certain significant details (for instance the folds and rippling edges of the chitons), they also display very different, sometimes frankly divergent characteristics. Thus the scenes are depicted with a formal rigorism, occasionally almost frigid in effect. The profiles, with their high foreheads, are unlike those usually found in Ionic art and indeed seem more in line with the graphic traditions of the pottery of the early archaic period in the Aegean islands. (However this tradition lingered on in East Greek communities until a quite late period.) The slab showing a goddess and a man with a scepter certainly belongs to this same tradition of forms, rendered with an improved technique, though it also has many affinities with Ionian delicacy and grace.

The connection between these paintings and the concepts behind the drawings on the Caeretan *hydriai* is relatively slender. Those vases, which nowadays are plausibly enough attributed to the *atelier* of an Ionian master who had migrated to and settled in Caere, are characterized by a rendering of bodies that is lively, dynamic and says much for the artist's sense of humor. This style directly corresponds to the art of the painted tombs of Tarquinii: especially the Tombs of the Augurs and of the Lionesses. However it is probable that painted slabs were produced at Caere which were stylistically closely akin to the art currents manifested in the Caeretan *hydriai* and, in a general way, to those stemming from northern Ionia and Aeolia. This is evidenced by the fragment of a slab in the Berlin Museum, showing a woman shaking hands with a man (whose form is missing), and a large bird. Fragments recently discovered at Caere are no less revealing : some formed part of what must have been a fair-sized frieze showing Perseus killing one of the Gorgons—which, for once anyhow, proves the mythological nature of the subjects of the slabs.

Finally, we have good reasons for believing that the output of the artists of Caere was shaped by greatly varying tendencies (perhaps under the direction of various foreign masters), and pertained to several schools ; hence the diversity we find in the productions of the indigenous artists. As for the Campana slabs and the fragment in Berlin, and those recently discovered, these may be roughly attributed to the penultimate decades of the sixth century B.C.

BACK WALL. TOMB OF THE AUGURS, TARQUINII.

TOMB OF THE AUGURS

A mysterious world of atavistic beliefs and dark sanguinary rites, charged with primitive, starkly physical ferocity, is revealed to us in the paintings of this small, lavishly decorated tomb of Tarquinii, in which, suitably enough, tones of red predominate. At the back, on either side of a painted door, which symbolizes the barrier between the living and the kingdom of death, two figures raise their arms in gestures of lament and salutation or farewell. On the sides, fierce, bloodthirsty funeral games are depicted with an almost overpowering realism. Here for the first time (round about 530 B.C., or a little later) we find a painter employing a theme that derived entirely from the Etruscan life of the day, with its own particular customs, its intense religious feeling combined with a materialistic outlook—which the Greeks found so baffling.

In the center of the right wall of the tomb two wrestlers are at grips. Their massive bodies lean towards each other, each man's left leg advanced, their heads so close that they almost touch. The younger, who is beardless, has already a firm hold on his adversary's wrists. Three bowls of different colors, one above the other, are placed between the two wrestlers, and perhaps represent the prize of the contest. An umpire, or *agonothetes*, presides over this match, which forms part of the funeral games. Clad in a cloak, he is coming from the left, one arm outstretched. He is carrying a *lituus*, or augur's crook, emblem of his office, and is followed by another equally dignified man, who is looking over his shoulder and gesturing to a little slave boy to make haste. The boy, who is carrying a folding stool, almost trips up over another little hooded slave squatting on the ground. Two red birds are flashing by over the wrestlers, a detail which once led to a misinterpretation of this scene, it being thought these men were augurs watching the flight of the birds. Hence the name, *Tomba degli Auguri*, by which the tomb is known.

The effect of strength produced by the bodies of the two athletes is quite astonishing and has no parallel in archaic art. The bulky limbs, the round massive heads, the men's locked posture and the geometrically precise balance of the composition contribute to giving the impression of two heavy masses poised against each other. There are obvious reminiscences of the corpulent figures found in Ionic drawings, such as the gigantic Herakles slaying King Busiris and his followers on the Caeretan *hydria* in the Museum of Vienna. It is even possible that the painter of the Tomb of the Augurs may, either directly or indirectly, have studied under East Greek masters working at Caere. Some aspects of the execution of the figures—the lines briefly indicating anatomical details, and the drawing of the round heads with their receding foreheads, big noses, thick lips and large staring eyes—show that this painting belongs to the same art current as the Caeretan *hydriai*.

It must, however, be remembered that in his frieze in the Tomb of the Augurs the painter has been obliged to abandon the traditional methods of handling mythological themes; though tradition allowed considerable latitude to the artist, the spirit and the manner of his representation were prescribed by custom. Here he was venturing into a quite new field; trying to body forth scenes which he had actually witnessed—all the more precisely and realistically inasmuch as the pictures were meant to have a concrete value as regards the after-life of the dead man. This was the attitude in which he approached his creative task. Here we have a case of real originality and inventiveness, a work that does not stem from any precedents, even though the painter drew inspiration for his forms and some of his types from previous pictures. This intense desire for total realism may explain certain characteristics which are far to seek in the mythological scenes on East Greek pottery; we have here an early token of the high originality of Ionico-Etruscan painting. The strongly characterized expression of material force which we find in the figures of the wrestlers is nothing short of brutal, and the same tendency towards vivid characterization is apparent, if in a different manner, in the picturesque, almost homely group of the two umpires and their small attendants.

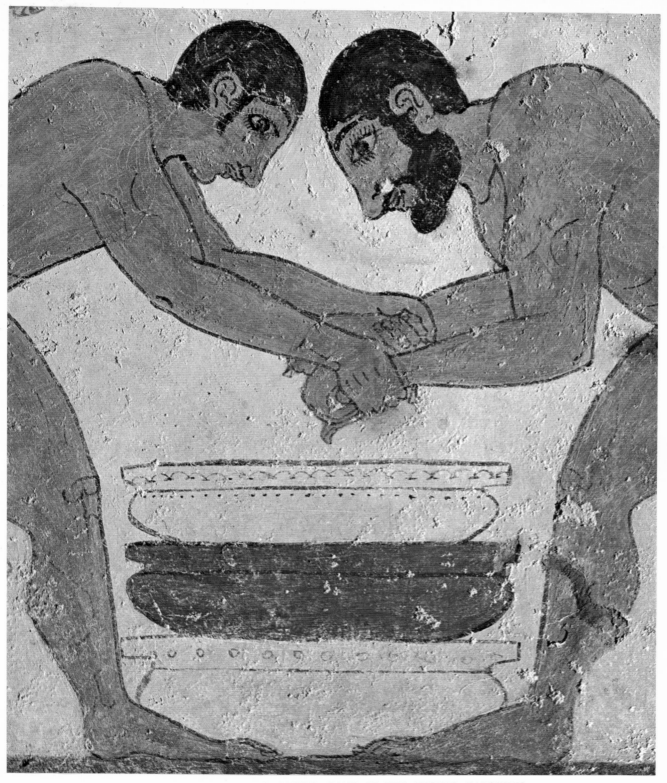

THE WRESTLERS, DETAIL. TOMB OF THE AUGURS, TARQUINII.

The evocative power of the frescos in the Tomb of the Augurs makes itself even more strongly felt in the scenes following those we have just described. Quite devoid of continuity, these succeed one another on the right wall of the tomb and reappear (though in a much more damaged state) on the left wall.

Two outlandish figures are engaged in combat. In the scene depicted on the right wall the first combatant is wearing only shorts, an abbreviated red tunic and a high pointed cap with a kind of striped visor in front; his features are hidden behind a darkish mask and a long beard, probably false. The inscription designates him by the name *phersu*, an Etruscan word corresponding to the Latin *persona* (meaning a masked man, an actor). This man is coming in from the right holding a rope, or leash, with which he has succeeded in entangling the legs and arms of his opponent; the end of the rope is attached to the collar of a dog, who has sunk his teeth into the left leg of the second figure. This man is naked except for a sash round his loins; his head is wrapped round with a white cloth. In his right hand he brandishes a club, but this too is entangled in the rope. The blood running from his wounds is indicated by the red brushstrokes on his body.

The same group appears again on the opposite wall along with other figures difficult to make out. But here the situation has taken a new turn; the masked man, now deprived of both dog and rope, is fleeing as fast as his legs can carry him, hotly pursued by his opponent. Looking back at his pursuer, he raises his right arm as if to ward off a blow. In this scene he wears no shorts. Though he is represented as thickset and burly, his gestures and attitude are rendered with much vivacity, and the impression of speed and movement is admirably conveyed.

Obviously we see here one of the funeral games associated with the ceremonial burials of antiquity; nothing similar to them has yet come to light anywhere else, except perhaps at Tarquinii in the so-called Tomb of the Punchinello, today in a badly damaged condition. But unlike the athletic contests, this is a fight to the death. The *phersu* defends himself with his dog and rope, while his opponent is armed with a club. The latter's life depends on his ability to bludgeon the dog and his master before being fatally enmeshed in the rope and torn to pieces by the animal. The origin and significance of this savage custom are hard to determine. It may quite possibly stem from very ancient sacrificial rites in which a human life was offered up to the deceased. We have evidence of such rites in prehistoric times and in proto-historic civilization in the East; historians agree, moreover, that ceremonies of this kind lie at the origin of the gladiatorial combats which arose in Campania—a region colonized by the Etruscans, be it noted—and which, even under the Roman Empire, were connected in some respects with funeral rites.

However this may be, the scenes of the *phersu* and his opponent engaged in a fight to the death in the Tomb of the Augurs bring out the realistic, indigenous characteristics of these Etruscan paintings. Indeed they have a savagery combined with reminiscences of ancient rites which differentiates them from the East Greek tradition and emphasizes their originality and singularity.

THE MASKED MAN RUNNING AWAY. TOMB OF THE AUGURS, TARQUINII.

The decorative elements (in the strict sense of the term) employed in the Tomb of the Augurs call for mention. Underneath the picture sequence of the frieze, which is set unusually high, is a red band and, below this, a black dado. On the back wall, frieze and dado are intersected by a painted door which narrows slightly towards the top, inset between broad red verticals (representing the door-jambs) and a lintel projecting on each side of these. The structure of the two-leaved door is indicated by three red horizontal bands, studded with painted orange-yellow disks like nail-heads, and traversed by a central vertical band, where the two leaves meet. Above the doorway and frieze runs a pattern of black, red and green stripes. The lower surface of the big longitudinal beam spanning the ceiling is painted, and its two sides ornamented with florets. On the pediment are a lion and a leopard attacking a goat. Particularly interesting are the various ways in which the artist has arranged the plant and bird motifs in the empty spaces between the figures of the frieze. (Such motifs became very popular elements in the frieze paintings of Etruscan tombs.) He sketched in the red birds directly without the use of preliminary contour-lines, and the effects these produce are at once varied and delightfully vivacious.

In the execution of the paintings the drawing naturally plays a leading part; it consists of preliminary incised lines and lines painted in black. These do not only indicate the outlines of the figures but are also used to delineate inner details, and include some discreet but precise indications of anatomical features. The color is applied in flat even tones on the areas within the contour-lines; brushwork, without preliminary contour-lines, is confined to the birds and the blue leaves of the shrubs. Traces of mixed color can be seen in the hair of one of the umpires. The predominating hues, those determining the color-scheme of the frieze, are white, black and red, a special, attenuated red being employed for the flesh tints. Yellow and two mixed colors, orange and brownish purple, are reserved for a few details; blue appears only in the leafage of the plants; green in one of the stripes of the band above the frieze.

BACK WALL, TOMB OF THE LIONESSES, TARQUINII.

TOMB OF THE LIONESSES

This belongs to a period slightly later than, and to the same artistic 'climate' as the Tomb of the Augurs (whose painter must undoubtedly have been trained in the school of East Greek artists which was then established and enjoying much success at Caere). Its approximate date would be 520 B.C. But the painter has taken more festive aspects of real life for his theme: banqueters reclining under a sort of portico or colonnaded pavilion. On the back wall we see musicians and dancers and in the center an enormous wine bowl wreathed with ivy. All these people display an almost orgiastic physical vitality which, strangely enough, does not clash with the essentially religious character of the occasion. The exuberant, joyous inspiration of the artist makes itself felt in the lavish decoration and the gaiety of the colors.

The Tomb of the Lionesses is one of the most impressive of the Tarquinii tombs owing to the richness of the decoration on the walls of the small sepulchral chamber, as well as to the excellent state of preservation of the vividly colored paintings.

The ceiling is decorated with a red longitudinal band imitating the lower surface of a central beam, with a motif of large white and red checks on the side courses. In the pediment two panthers (not lionesses) face each other, separated by a painted pilaster represented as supporting the roof and crowned with volutes. We see here the typical, traditional lay-out of the decorations on the pediments of Etruscan painted tombs. This arrangement of animals facing each other often figured on the pediments of the earliest Greek buildings and also on the façades of the rock-tombs of Asia Minor. Here it seems to indicate the belated persistance of a very ancient architectural motif that had been used in decorations of the Aegean world since time immemorial; harking back, indeed, to the Mycenaean civilization, as is evidenced by the famous bas-relief on the Lion Gate at Mycenae.

On either side of the doors and in the center of the side walls six full-length columns are painted; they are of the proto-Doric or Tuscan type with a base, a smooth red-brown shaft, a capital with a black band, a green or blue neck, a bulging red-brown echinus and brown abacus. The presence of these columns shows that the decorator of the tomb intended to imitate on the side walls a porticoed building or pavilion. Beneath this four big male figures are reclining at a banquet. The back wall, however, is decorated with an enormous scene of song and dance, with smaller figures. A large wine-bowl is placed in the center wreathed with ivy-leaves and flanked by the two traditional Etruscan musicians: the lyre-player and the double-pipe player. Round this group the dancers disport themselves: a man and woman on the right, a sumptuously clad dancing-girl on the left. On the ground, in the right-hand corner, stands a black jar.

The figured frieze occupies the upper part of the walls and is edged at the bottom by a sumptuous cornice of palmettes and lotus flowers. On the dado below is a seascape with the waves painted in grey-violet. Dolphins are leaping across the waves and above them birds are flying, rhythmically alternating with the dolphins. This sea motif, though its conception is essentially decorative, has realistic aspects foreshadowing the great landscape painting in the second chamber of the Tomb of Hunting and Fishing. A rectangular niche, set off by a small painted architrave which interrupts the palmette cornice, opens into the center of the back wall. This was most likely intended to contain the urn with the ashes of the deceased.

The elements of the composition can in all probability be interpreted in the light of this last mentioned feature of the tomb, which suggests that it was built for a single person, who favored the funerary rite of cremation. Thus the large *crater* in the center of the frieze obviously represents the cinerary urn, on either side of which musicians play, placed like the mourners on either side of the door in the Tomb of the Augurs; an arrangement exactly paralleled in other monuments (e.g. in the later Tomba della Pulcella for instance). The black jar is probably the vessel containing the water for extinguishing the pyre. The dance and banquet form part of the funeral ceremony.

RITUAL DANCE. TOMB OF THE LIONESSES, TARQUINII.

What extraordinary vitality there is in this dance for the dead! The dancers face each other, echoing each other's gestures in the rushing rhythms of the *tripudium*. One foot strikes the ground while the other leg is jerked upwards. One arm is raised and the other lowered. The body of the completely naked youth on the right is painted brick-red, his long fair hair is fringed with curls above his forehead and ripples down his chest and behind his shoulders. He holds a metal *olpe*, or jug, in his left hand. The woman, whose flesh is colored pinkish-white, only wears a thin, transparent chiton and her black hair is gathered into a knot. The lower hem of the billowing chiton with its well-marked folds is the only passage in the composition in which a pure red pigment has been employed. She is playing the castanets with her lowered right hand, while holding up her left with the fingers forked, in a curiously intriguing, probably ritual gesture.

A single dancer balances the pair on the other side of the wine-bowl. Unlike them she is magnificently dressed. Her head is covered by a *tutulus*, the characteristic elongated Ionic cap, made of orange-red material dotted with little flowers; she wears a large round earring; her long, full chiton with short pointed sleeves is made of the same material as the *tutulus* and piped with red at the hem; a large brick-red mantle with wide blue lappets is thrown over her chiton; her elegant pointed shoes are also brick-red. The dance rhythm is conveyed by the wide step and flexible movement of the arms and legs.

Notice how the soft forms, the eurythmic composition, the bright yet even coloring give this figure a quite amazing decorative value. The bell-shaped cloak floats like an involucrum round the soft, vibrant body and, in fanning out towards the bottom forms as it were a large inverted lotus, like the hanging lotus flowers in the decorative band underneath the picture. Can this be no more than a happy coincidence ? The harmony of form and color that exists between the figure of the dancing-girl and the decorative elements of the border (a pattern of myrtle leaves, palmettes and lotus flowers) can be seen in our subsequent plate, which includes the border in question. Indeed the painter's fine feeling for ornament binds together, to wonderful effect, the scene depicted on the frieze and the architectural and decorative elements.

A sense of physical reality and movement, on the other hand, characterizes the drawing of the figures. Both the dancing couple and the separate girl have soft, amply molded limbs which none the less are taut and supple, rather squat bodies, large heads, rounded profiles with sloping foreheads and pointed noses. Yet, despite the ingenuousness of the archaic conventions (profile, heads and legs combined with definitely frontal busts), the attitudes are vivacious, full of character and charm. Here we have no difficulty in recognizing the peculiar imprint of East Greek art, above all as elaborated in the centers of the Aeolian Islands and of southern Asiatic Ionia, as we see it, for instance, in the bas-relief frieze of Larissa, in the painted pottery of Kyme or, in Etruria itself, in the Caeretan *hydriai*. Of all the monuments of Ionico-Etruscan painting perhaps the Tomb of the Lionesses can be considered most representative of this particular trend in the currents of East Greek art, where humor and dynamism prevail over the languid grace of the pictorial art of South Ionia (Samos for instance).

Whatever his origin may have been, the painter of this tomb must have worked rapidly, making his observations and composing directly from the life, in a mood of gay, indeed untrammelled brio, all the more remarkable considering the funerary associations of the subject-matter. The immediacy and spontaneity of his creative impulse are indicated by the anomalies of the graffito lines and even of the colored contours (particularly noticeable in the face and cap of the dancing-girl). In the female figures a thicker red-brown line sometimes accompanies or even replaces the black outline. For the first time the color, which is applied regularly and evenly within the demarcated sectors, shows a very varied scale. In a range of simple and mixed tints, the painter has employed the following tonalities: white, black, grey, violet-grey, rose-white, red-brown, bright red, orange, brick-red, brown-red, blue and green.

WOMAN DANCING. TOMB OF THE LIONESSES, TARQUINII.

It is an interesting point that the banqueters figuring on the side walls of the Tomb of the Lionesses are given proportions strikingly larger than those of the musicians and dancers portrayed on the back wall. The former are probably members of the family of the dead man and their size is graded according to their importance, following a convention widely diffused in the primitive art of the Eastern Mediterranean; thus we have here an obvious sign of the persistence of archaism in the inspiration of this set of paintings. This disproportion is glaringly evident in the tiny attendant waiting upon one of the reclining figures. The majestic pose, the softness of the flowing outlines, the skillful rendering of facial expressions, the large patches of intense color, the vivacious effect of the bright locks of hair and of the looped bands hanging from nails in the ceiling, give these pictures an unmistakable character of their own, and we are justified in ranking them among the finest creations of all Ionico-Etruscan painting.

A BANQUETER. TOMB OF THE LIONESSES, TARQUINII.

BIRDS IN FLIGHT. TOMB OF HUNTING AND FISHING, TARQUINII.

THE TOMB OF HUNTING AND FISHING

In the Tomb of Hunting and Fishing at Tarquinii we have one of the most significant and suggestive manifestations of the pictorial art of the Mediterranean world during the archaic period. The tomb is divided into two rooms, the walls of which are completely covered with paintings. A merry festival with music and dancing is illustrated in the frieze of the first room; in the pediment is a scene of the return from the hunt. The walls of the second room are adorned with a quite remarkable landscape frieze depicting episodes of life at sea, while the pediment represents a family banquet. Notable here is the unusual variety of inspiration; alongside traditional formulas, such as the use of violently contrasting, non-naturalistic colors, we find daring and sophisticated innovations in the drawing, due probably to realistic observation by the artist. On stylistic grounds we are inclined to date this decoration somewhere around 520-510 B.C.

YOUTH DIVING FROM A ROCK. TOMB OF HUNTING AND FISHING, TARQUINII.

Beneath the festive chaplets, hung up as decorations of the house, the walls of the mortuary chamber are to be imagined as opening out upon a vast expanse of sea. Nature is represented in all the exuberance of her ever-changing forms, and if man has a share in these, he has here no pretensions to supremacy. A steep rock rises from the waves; its stratification seems to have made a vivid impression on the painter, and he has represented it in undulating stripes of different colors. A few scraggy bushes are growing on its sides, and to these a boy in a blue shirt is clinging as he clambers up the cliff, while on the other side another boy, who is naked, dives into the sea. This quite amazing realism is unique in all archaic art. The artist has not only painted a human figure upside-down, he has actually *watched* his model dive, and depicted almost photographically the characteristic position of the arms and legs, and the effect of gravity on a person falling headlong. And all around, the sky is dappled with many-colored birds.

The tale continues, and now we are shown a youth, painted on a larger scale and wearing a jacket and shorts, standing on a rock and aiming at birds with a sling. At the foot of the rock is a boat with a " lucky eye " painted on the prow and four people in it. The man at the helm and one of his companions are waving to the slinger, while another points towards the fourth man, in the prow, who is fishing with a line. Two wear short tunics and the other two are naked. A fat dolphin is turning a somersault on the waves. The air is thick with sea birds, perhaps wild duck—the dominant motif of the frieze. It is noteworthy that, whereas the figures and objects are delineated in the normal way with clean-cut black contour lines, the surface of the sea is rendered with a haze of broken colors, all in undulations, expressive of the ceaseless movement of the waves. That bluish-purple color is a most suitable pictorial equivalent of the Homeric epithet: ὄινοπα πόντον (usually translated " wine-dark sea "). The schematized non-realism of the colors, sometimes muted and blended, but oftener unmixed and bright, is specially noticeable in the birds, which are white, yellow, red, blue and green, and in the strata of the rock rendered in bands of grey, blue-purple, reddish and blue tints.

HUNTING AND FISHING. TOMB OF HUNTING AND FISHING, TARQUINII.

Whoever conceived the idea of these paintings in the Tomb of Hunting and Fishing must certainly have been a man of high originality. Such is the medley of themes figuring in the two chambers of this tomb that at first sight it seems difficult to determine what guided the artist in his choice of subjects. However, this becomes fairly clear if, so to speak, we mentally re-arrange the compositions on the two pediments and those on the walls. The banquet obviously goes with the dance scene, while the return from the hunt is logically connected with the hunting and fishing scenes. These last are undoubtedly pleasurable episodes taken from life, perhaps from the young days of the owner of the tomb or some member of his family, whom we may recognize in the largest figure, the youth who is plying a sling, almost in the center of the landscape frieze on the back wall of the second chamber.

In the decorations in the Tomb of Hunting and Fishing we find a range of themes not only remarkably varied but completely new to Etruscan painting. The outstanding characteristic of these scenes, from the compositional angle, is the reduction of the human figure to one of the elements of a wide over-all rendering of nature. We can see this process at work in the much damaged frieze on the walls of the first room. Here the musicians and dancers are smaller than the intervening trees, and in this scene of village festivity, details of the landscape are made to play an important part. The tendency to give pre-eminence to the landscape setting is even more apparent in the seascape of the inner room. We have here a work that is unique in the painting of the archaic and classical periods. There are two possible explanations; it may express the personal taste of a highly original Ionico-Etruscan artist, or else it may have been inspired by East Greek models, that is to say an artistic environment which, owing to contacts with oriental influences and ancient art traditions of the Aegean area that had lingered on, sponsored a type of landscape painting unknown to countries lying within the sphere of Greek archaism.

Among the unique features of the decoration and composition in the painting of this tomb, which point to the presence of new, specific foreign currents, are the scenes figuring in the small pediments. These are adjusted to the triangular setting and replace the usual pattern of two animals facing each other on either side of a pilaster. We have here a method of decorating pediments which became generalized in Greece —in the carved pedimental reliefs, anyhow—during the last quarter of the sixth century B.C. However, in the Tomb of Hunting and Fishing the uniqueness of the style of the paintings is due to the wonderful lifelikeness of the little figures; they have been observed and represented in every possible attitude, and are almost wholly uninfluenced by traditional procedures. Obviously the prevailing atmosphere is that of East Greek art; nevertheless the freedom of the drawing and the boldness of the rendering make us feel that we have here an independent, not to say revolutionary, painter, gifted with a spontaneous creative zest that prevailed against his cultural background. This explains the audacities of the drawing and the vivid unrealistic colors, characteristic of the painting of an earlier age. We find here the same range of colors as in the Tomb of the Lionesses, but with some interesting innovations as regards the blending of tones.

DANCERS. TOMB OF THE BACCHANTS, TARQUINII.

TOMB OF THE BACCHANTS

This is a quite small sepulchral chamber with much damaged frescos, and only a few isolated figures painted in yellow, red and black upon a large white ground. But though relatively unpretentious, the so-called Tomb of the Bacchants has certain characteristics that are of particular value for the appraisal of the archaic painting at Tarquinii. It was decorated by an artist with a strong feeling for line and an expert, refined touch, and he has created images at once fascinatingly delicate and full of movement. The festive scene and the arrangement of the figures anticipate the frieze of the Tomb of the Baron, though in an entirely different vein. Its date is about the same as that of the Tomb of Hunting and Fishing.

Beneath the ceiling painted with circles, ivy leaves and small flowers, stands a pediment with a central voluted pilaster and an animal on each side, depicting a lion savaging a terrified gazelle; this is one of the most delightful illustrations of the keen perceptiveness and adroitness with which Etruscan decorators could register, or invent, the attitudes of animals. The figured frieze beneath it takes up nearly the whole height of the walls. It contains scenes of music and dancing with figures or groups of figures between shrubs. At the back, on the right, a bearded man embraces an elegant young woman wearing a *tutulus*, perhaps the personages to whom the tomb was dedicated; on the left a dancing musician is holding a lyre upside down. On the right wall is a player on the double-lyre; on the left wall a group of dancers.

The artist who decorated the Tomb of the Bacchants proved himself an able and ingenious draftsman not only in the principal group on the back wall, where the soft delicacy of the markedly conventional Ionico-Etruscan female figure contrasts with the massive dynamism of the male figure. But it is above all in his rendering of the wild youths dancing naked, that he makes us conscious of his superb craftsmanship, so effectively does he depict the red-brown forms capering and gesticulating in a state of uncontrollable excitement. The color, dimmed to a mere shadow of itself, is merely accessory to the drawing; nevertheless, so happily inspired is the latter that this loss is hardly felt.

GAZELLE ATTACKED BY A LION. TOMB OF THE BACCHANTS, TARQUINII.

TOMB OF THE BARON

As far as can be judged from the surviving monuments, the Ionico-Etruscan phase at Tarquinii reaches its full stylistic maturity in the Tomb of the Baron. It is a little later than the Tomb of Hunting and Fishing, and like this last and the Tomb of the Bacchants, its frieze depicts a series of cheerful activities having no apparent reference to religion or to death. But here the artist's creative imagination has taken a very different course from that which was followed in the Tomb of Hunting and Fishing. He has not tried to achieve a meticulous description of reality or to fill the picture space with a crowd of people and landscape details. Quite otherwise, these paintings seem intended to stress the aristocratic eminence and isolation of the human element in a composition that reveals a highly cultured sense of rhythm.

The painter of the Tomb of the Baron belonged to the last generation of the sixth century, to that advanced phase of Ionico-Etruscan taste in which ideals of refinement and elegance began to supersede the vital, forceful art deriving from early East Greek influences, and which culminated, round about 500 B.C., in manneristic displays of graceful virtuosity.

The inspiration of these paintings stems from late Ionic art currents, indications of which can be found in pottery and in work of an analagous technique (e.g. the sarcophagi of Clazomenae and a recently published Ionic *hydria* of Caere which has somewhat different characteristics from the famous Caeretan *hydriai* series). It also, however, shows affinities with the style of Attic vase-painting in its early red-figured phase, and especially with the style of Epiktetos and Oltos. Its direct association with the latter would point to about 510 B.C. or a little later as being its probable date. Quite possibly the artist was a Greek painter visiting or settled in Etruria (as some have maintained on rather slender grounds), or else a culturally very up-to-date Etruscan. Actually the scheme of the decoration (with a tall-figured frieze and the traditional pedimental ornamentation of a pilaster and facing animals), together with the realistic treatment of the subjects, falls into line with the regular development of Tarquinian tomb painting.

The peculiarities, which we need not hesitate to attribute to the inventiveness and personal inspiration of the decorator, lie in the technique and style. The artist has painted directly upon the smoothed-out rock-face in an unusual manner, that is to say without any plaster undercoat. He has traced out the approximate forms—as it were the shadows of his figures and plants—and even the borders of the frieze, with a grey, soft band of color, and then proceeded to delineate contours with the usual dark line, which here, however, is exceptionally fine and often completely submerged by the paint applied thereafter. This is of a thick, spongy texture, easily absorbed by the porous, granulated surface of the rock, and exceptionally bright. He built up the following color scale, starting out from basic tones of white (never used in its pure state): red, black and green (the absence of blue is noteworthy), light grey, dark grey, black, brick-red, purple-brown and green. The solidity and vigor of the colors, especially in the large range of reds used for the flesh tints and the cloaks, and of the blacks and reds for the bodies of the horses, tend almost to obliterate the interior details and also cause the dark forms of the figures to stand out in strong relief against the light ground of the rock. We may feel inclined to wonder whether the artist intended to carry his work a stage farther and eliminate the effect of unfinish produced by the greyish haloes and by the way the color blots out contour-lines, or whether he regarded the results of this way of painting as definitive.

In any case the originality of the technique stresses the formal innovations of these paintings, in which the artist seems to have converted the set subject into a purely stylistic fantasy of rhythm and color. The composition of the frieze consists of a succession of elegant upright human figures, horses and horsemen, spaced out on an empty white ground, symmetrically arranged and interspersed here and there with the tender

PROFFERING THE CUP. TOMB OF THE BARON, TARQUINII.

green of shrubs. In depicting his figures the painter seems to forget for the nonce his virtuosity in the medium of representation and, instead, to concentrate upon an abstract rendering of slender, elongated forms stripped down to essentials, implemented by well-contrived effects of color.

The most conspicuous subject figures on the back wall. A bearded man of noble mien, in a black cloak bordered with grey, stands with his arm round a youth wearing a thin grey mantle who is playing on the double pipes, while with his left hand he is proffering a cup to a woman with a high *tutulus* on her head over which is draped a red mantle. This almost homely scene recalls, or may serve as a substitute for the traditional banquet. Perhaps it is meant specially to do honor to the lady, who may be the wife of the bearded man or mother of the youths who appear on this as well as on the other walls, and for whom the tomb may have been prepared and decorated owing to her having died before the other members of the family.

This is the left wall of the tomb. Two youths, each raising an arm and pointing with one finger, have just dismounted and are speaking to an elaborately dressed woman wearing a *tutulus* who stands between them. The dresses, mantles and pointed shoes of the youths and the *tutulus*, mantle, chiton and shoes of the lady are painted in bright tones of purple, red, green and grey, which harmonize completely with the red of the male figures' flesh and the grey of the women's, the black of the women's hair and the grey of the youths', the red and black of the horses' bodies and the grey of their manes and tails. The wonderfully successful effect of this composition is due to the skillfully balanced symmetry of the figures, and the slightly pyramidal structure of the scene resulting from the converging angles of the slanting silhouettes, directed upwards towards the center, and the raised arms of the youths. This centering movement is implemented by the necks and hind quarters of the horses. But its effectiveness is due above all to the strongly architectonic treatment of the living forms and the way in which the colors match and second it. Notice (above all in the detail reproduced on the cover of this volume) how the painter has visualized these figures as incarnations of his own, very personal and sophisticated ideal of long-limbed elegance and constructive color. Except for an attempt to render the foreshortening of bodies seen in profile (the so-called "obliqua imago"), the bodily structure of the figures is wholly devoid of any kind of concrete corporeality; so much so that the thickly applied color is allowed to encroach upon and even obscure the shape of the front part of the body.

CONVERSATION PIECE. TOMB OF THE BARON, TARQUINII.

2

THE MASTERS OF THE SEVERE STYLE

(FIFTH CENTURY B.C.)

During the late archaic period, towards the end of the sixth century, a thorough-going change came over ancient art. The Greek artists took a passionate interest in Man, since, for them, Man was the measure of all things, and applied themselves to studying the human figure with the curiosity of naturalists, and to rendering attitudes of rest and movement according to the laws of foreshortening. The effects of this far-reaching change, which certainly had its beginnings in painting, are most clearly to be seen in the red-figured Attic pottery of the severe style, during the period between the death of Peisistratus and the end of the Persian wars (528-480 B.C.).

Inevitably Etruria was affected by this movement. Indeed, thanks to the happy chance that the Etruscan monumental paintings have survived, we may go so far as to say that it is in Etruria—and in Etruria alone—that we can discern its salient characteristics and judge of its most significant manifestations, especially as regards the handling of color.

However, the religious or practical considerations guiding the artists who made the decorations of the Etruscan tombs and those who commissioned them did not change with the transition from the Ionico-Etruscan phase in painting to that of the severe style. The subjects, taken from or inspired by real life, remained essentially the same, as against the mythological themes prevailing in Greek figure painting. For this reason Etruscan painting tended to develop on lines of its own during this period and artists emerged with strongly defined personalities, such as that of the painter of the Tomb of the Triclinium; in fact a number of works of art of very high quality and of unquestionable originality were now produced.

As a result of the prestige of the masters of the severe style, their language became what was in effect a national tradition during the whole of the fifth century—as is evidenced by the long series of tombs at Tarquinii and Chiusi. Historical events contri-buted to this result. For, owing to the grave political and economic crisis which befell

Etruria at this time, the active trade and cultural relations with Greece which had flourished during the previous period gradually diminished. Thus Etruria remained practically isolated from and unaffected by the stylistic revolution of the century of Polygnotos and Pheidias: that is to say the creation of classical art.

Poverty, isolation and the lack of an innate capacity for self-development account for the decline and the almost complete cessation of Etruscan pictorial productivity during the second half of the fifth century and the first half of the fourth.

HORSE. TOMB OF THE CHARIOTS, TARQUINII.

TOMB OF THE CHARIOTS

The paintings of this tomb, which were badly damaged and threatened with irreparable destruction, have been lifted and re-assembled in the Museum of Tarquinia. They have much significance as regards the history of the development of Etruscan painting. The sepulchral chamber, which is relatively large, is decorated with two superimposed figured friezes, one with athletic contests on a white ground and the other with a banquet and dancing on a red ground. The change in the artistic taste of the period is evident in the upper frieze which shows the influence of Greek, and more particularly Attic models of the end of the sixth and the beginning of the fifth century. The execution of these paintings can be dated around the year 490 B.C.

ATHLETES AND HORSEMAN. TOMB OF THE CHARIOTS, TARQUINII.

The upper frieze runs along a raised band spanning the wall. It has a great number of small figures in all sorts of attitudes, and supplies the most complete documentation we possess of the various games and athletic exercises, sometimes of an exciting and spectacular order, at a great Etruscan funeral: chariot races, feats of horsemanship, wrestling, boxing, jumping, javelin and discus hurling, military dances and the like. The games are held in the area of a field or of a stadium, lined with stands (represented on the frieze in the corners of the wall) for the spectators, who eagerly watch and discuss the games, while a motley crowd, depicted in realistic attitudes, lounges beneath the stands. In this detail of the frieze, on the back wall, two naked athletes are seen in repose, while another wearing a helmet is mounted on a little blue horse. It is interesting to notice that in the preliminary design the profile of another horse was outlined at the back, together with the leg of the horseman; this, however, has been effaced by the coloring.

This is another detail of the small frieze, and is on the left wall of the tomb. The little dancer, armed with a helmet and shield and carrying a twisted lance, is perhaps a *ludio*, engaged in one of those comic imitations of the sacred warrior dances the tradition of which was later transmitted to Roman ceremonies from the Etruscan repertory. On the left are two athletes in repose and a discobolus. The drawing of these figures, traced both with graffito and painted lines, clearly indicates the emergence of a new stylistic program, as regards the painting of the Ionico-Etruscan phase. Their proportions are elegant and slender. The attitudes and gestures demonstrate the artist's intelligent observation of anatomical structure and of movement, particularly the movements of the male body in the palaestra. Specially significant are the bold foreshortenings in which he manifests a fixed determination to supersede the conventions of archaic art.

ATHLETES AND ARMED DANCER. TOMB OF THE CHARIOTS, TARQUINII.

The Tomb of the Chariots must certainly have been decorated by an outstanding artist, for some particularly rich family of refined taste. It is remarkable not only for the splendor of its decoration, but also for the delicacy of the technique and the novelty of the style. Unfortunately the damaged state in which it is today, 125 years after its discovery, prevents us from forming more than a summary idea of these qualities.

The decoration, both ornamental and figured, completely covers all the surface of the large burial chamber. The pediment shows the normal arrangement of a central pilaster shaped as an altar; but it differs from the usual scheme with facing animals owing to the presence of human figures: two large figures of youths reclining on either side, and two other small nudes standing in front of a wine-bowl painted on the pilaster. On the back wall the large frieze represents a triclinium with male couples reclining on couches and figures of male attendants. The representation of the banquet continues on the right wall with a table set with several vessels. As for the rest of the decoration, a sequence of dancing youths and maidens (alternating with bushes), some of them also playing musical instruments, is painted on the side walls. It is noteworthy that the women still wear the Etruscan cap known as the *tutulus*, whereas the men have already adopted the fashion of short hair.

The technical processes employed by the artist have been elucidated after the careful examination carried out at the time the paintings were lifted. Implemented by the quality of the plaster, which contains vegetable elements, the delicacy of the drawing of the contours is particularly noticeable; and the figures are already fitted neatly, with a sure hand, within the graffito guide lines. The range of basic colors seems more restricted, as against those of the more noteworthy tombs preceding and following it: thus yellow and green are lacking. This may suggest a deliberate sobriety in the use of color, bearing out the theory that the artist was mainly concerned with the drawing, and this would be in accord with the style of the presumed Attic models. The meticulous craftsmanship of the painter is also indicated by his use of different whites and reds for the figures from those of the grounds of the two friezes.

Apart from monuments of Attic bas-relief, such as the base of the wall of Themistocles with athletic scenes, the pictures in the Tomb of the Chariots, and especially those of the athletes, have their most obvious and direct parallel in Attic red-figured vases of the Euphronios and Euthymides type. This not only holds good for the outline of each individual figure, with its stiff, tense, yet naturally poised construction, without precedent in Etruscan painting; it also applies to the over-all composition of the small frieze. Indeed it seems to move away from the ideals of Ionico-Etruscan art, so as to come into line with the severe ambiance of the palaestra, where, in accordance with the Hellenic spirit, interest is focused on the idealized human figure. The lower frieze, on the other hand, appears to be more closely assimilated to traditional conceptions and forms, on almost manneristic lines. All these circumstances point to a desire and a capacity for innovation on the part of the painter of the Tomb of the Chariots, whether he was Greek or Etruscan, though these innovating tendencies still are tempered by the conventions of Etruscan figurative art.

WRESTLERS. TOMB OF THE MONKEY, CHIUSI.

TOMB OF THE MONKEY

The tomb painting of Chiusi began in the fifth century and it was associated with the period of political and cultural prosperity which this city, situated in the interior of the Etruscan territory, was then enjoying. By and large it belongs to the phase of the " severe style." Of the surviving monuments, the Tomb of the Monkey, though not in very good condition, is certainly the most interesting. It has a central chamber with three chambers opening round it, and a coffered ceiling. A small figured frieze (interrupted by the doors) depicting athletic contests, race-course scenes and spectators, runs round the walls of the central chamber. In the back chamber there are slight traces of other paintings. The ceiling, too, is painted with ornamental and figure motifs (female heads seen front view, harpies). The style, while showing signs of the innovations of late archaic art as reflected in the Tomb of the Chariots at Tarquinii, comprises forms which, if rather provincial, have nevertheless much vivacity. A somewhat later date must, however, be assigned: somewhere around 480-470 B.C.

Here, as in the small frieze of the Tomb of the Chariots, funerary games seem to constitute an independent theme sufficient to itself. The usual representation of a banquet is missing (there is just a timid suggestion of small figures of attendants in the back cell). It is, however, quite possible that in the noble lady wearing a *tutulus* and mantle, who is represented sitting under a sunshade at the beginning of the frieze on the right of the entrance wall, we have the likeness of a real person, perhaps the deceased. She is evidently watching the games. In front of her, behind a kind of raised, decorated podium, is a flute-player with a large-brimmed hat; a girl in a jacket balancing an object like a candelabrum on her head is dancing to his accompaniment. These are doubtless jugglers. This scene, unique in Etruscan painting, is extraordinarily vivid and convincing.

The games are of the " agonistic " kind, and on the whole recapitulate the repertory of the Tomb of the Chariots, with the difference that here a countrified atmosphere seems to replace that of the Greek palaestra and stadium. There are several riding contests. Strongly characterized and comic figures mingle with the athletes. From the point of view of composition and typology, we may note such bold, photographically depicted groups as the wrestler flinging his adversary over his shoulder in the presence of an umpire with his hand raised. The free, unconstrained movements of the heads and legs of the galloping horses are well rendered. The bodies of the athletes, however, are not slim as those in the Tomb of the Chariots, and the heads of the figures are proportionately larger. Outlines are strongly emphasized.

Painting at Chiusi seems to have followed for the most part uniform directives and lay-outs during the whole course of its development, so far as can be judged by the existing works and by reproductions of those that have perished. In fact we have an impression of far greater uniformity, when we compare this art with that of Tarquinii; this seems to point to the existence of only one local school of painting, which was little affected by outside influences. The date of the Tomb of Orpheus and Eurydice (which no longer exists), where there were also scenes of music and dancing between shrubs, may probably be fixed a little earlier. On the other hand the Tomb of the Hill or the Two Chariots, where the pictures have survived and show a banqueting scene with games, is later. It is difficult to fix the chronology of the similar figure-paintings known to us by watercolors and drawings, which show but few variations of the usual motifs. It may, however, be assumed that this school continued to flourish throughout the fifth century, to the end of which belong the few much damaged fragments of battle-scenes from the Paolozzi Tomb, now in the Museum of Chiusi.

At Chiusi the paintings are closely connected, so far as subject and style are concerned, with the art of the funerary reliefs on contemporary gravestones and urns.

OWING TO THE IMPRACTICABILITY OF ILLUMINATING THE SUBJECT IN THIS TOMB SUFFICIENTLY.
THE PHOTOGRAPH HERE IS SOMEWHAT LESS PERFECT THAN THE OTHERS

BANQUET SCENE, DETAIL. TOMB OF THE LEOPARDS, TARQUINII.

TOMB OF THE LEOPARDS

The decoration of the fifth-century tombs of Tarquinii seems during a certain period to conform to a well-established, standardized lay-out, with a banqueting scene on the back wall and scenes of dancing and music-making on the side walls. This lay-out had already made its appearance towards the end of the Ionico-Etruscan period (e.g. in the Tomb of the Painted Vases) and in the lower frieze of the Tomb of the Chariots. A characteristic example, in very good condition, of this can be seen in the Tomb of the Leopards which, on the strength of certain typological analogies with Attic vase-painting, may be assigned to approximately the decade 480-470 B.C. Here the influence of the Greek severe style is apparent, but also an attempt to express character and movement, and an effective use of brilliant color.

SERVANT CARRYING A WINE BOWL. TOMB OF THE LEOPARDS, TARQUINII.

The Tomb of the Leopards is a small sunk chamber with brightly colored, remarkably well preserved frescos, and is one of the monuments that most impress the average

PLAYER ON THE DOUBLE PIPES. TOMB OF THE LEOPARDS, TARQUINII.

visitor to the necropolis of Tarquinii. For these reasons, rather than for the quality of
the work itself, some comment on it seems called for.

A single figured frieze runs round the chamber, up to a considerable height along the walls. The back wall shows a triclinium with young couples reclining on three festal couches: a man and woman on the central couch and on the one to the right, and two men on the left. The men have black, and the women fair hair, which, since these figures obviously represent the members of the family to whom the tomb belonged, may perhaps be a realistic detail—i.e. true to life, rather than a fashion or a figurative convention such as the difference in the flesh tints—of which there are no other existing examples. All wear myrtle wreaths, and bright mantles with large borders cover the naked bodies of the men and the chitons of the women. Between the couches young attendants are serving the banqueters. Laurel bushes are painted beneath and behind the couches. Along the side walls figures of servants and musicians advance towards the triclinium, spaced out between laurel bushes. The movements of the figures on the right wall suggest that they are footing a dance-step; some are looking back. Those on the left, however, are all shown in profile and moving forward with ordered, tranquil steps. The part of the fresco near the entrance door of the tomb is almost totally destroyed.

The decoration over the frieze is of much interest. On the pediment the two leopards which give the tomb its name confront each other according to the ancient traditional lay-out, but without the central supporting pilaster. The beam of the ceiling is painted with concentric circles, the sides have a checkered pattern; all are treated in bright colors.

The manner of dressing the hair and the clothes worn by the people here represented show a slightly more advanced mode than that exemplified in the paintings of the Tomb of the Chariots. The female fashion of wearing a veiled *tutulus* seems to have completely disappeared. The long flowing hair is reserved, and then only exceptionally, for the attendants. Obviously fashions diffused from Greek centers during the Persian wars had by now completely ousted the Ionic style of dress, even in Etruria. The drawing, which betokens the direct and widespread influence of late archaic Attic models, with slight reminiscences of traditional formulas inherited from Ionico-Etruscan schools, is also in keeping with these iconographic characteristics.

On the other hand the technique of the frescos does not reveal any real novelty as regards the archaic series of tombs at Tarquinii. The graffito preparation is quite visible; the outlined inner details of the figures are clearly marked; the colors are evenly laid on. In the execution of the work as a whole, easy, simple and even shoddy methods can be detected, which contrast with the general level of the technique and refinement of earlier (and also some contemporary) tomb paintings. The outlines are of different thicknesses, and sometimes irregular and wavering. The basic colors (white, black, yellow, red, blue and green) are applied without half-tones or blendings, except for the pink-white of the female flesh tints and the red-brown of the male. There is only occasional evidence (in the hair and in the leaves of the bushes) of large strokes showing traces of diluted color.

Upon a careful examination of the composition, the drawing of the figures, the use and distribution of the colors, and the technical details of the decoration of the Tomb of the Leopards, the unusually poor conception and execution of the painting

HEAD OF THE LYRE-PLAYER, DETAIL. TOMB OF THE LEOPARDS, TARQUINII.

becomes all too evident, once the first impression given by the excellent preservation of the pictures has worn off. For the first time in Etruscan tomb painting the work of a somewhat unschooled painter of limited genius, faced with a more difficult task than he is qualified to tackle, is presented in a striking manner for our evaluation.

The introduction into Etruria of the new Greek stylistic formulas of the end of the sixth and beginning of the fifth century, as seen in the Tomb of the Chariots, must certainly have involved a considerable change of outlook in the local taste, for which not a few of the Etruscan artists, and especially the professional painters, found themselves unprepared. The decoration of the Tomb of the Leopards is a significant example of the way in which the artisans of Tarquinii reacted to the artistic tendencies that were developing during the first years of the century. Actually it presupposes the existence of models the stylistic quality of which was at least equal to that of the Tomb of the Chariots, in one or more of the vanished tombs ; these presumably suggested this lay-out of the triclinium at the back with rows of attendants, musicians and dancers along the side walls. Another instance of the employment of these models will be seen in the stupendous composition of the frieze in the Tomb of the Triclinium, which was, however, slightly more recent and more highly developed than the presumed prototypes of the Tomb of the Leopards.

The painter of this last tomb shows himself fundamentally incapable of handling the techniques of perspective and movement implicit in the figures he sets out to imitate. His men and women are often stunted and ungainly, with short bodies, large heads, legs badly placed beneath the drapery—as in the case of the attendant advancing with a drinking-bowl and looking over his shoulder. The player on the double pipes who follows, taking large strides, has his left shoulder drawn in a straight line with his chest, in an unsuccessful attempt at foreshortening, and enormous arms and hands; the flung-back mantle is depicted in a confused way, with incongruous, superimposed outlines and stripes of color. The anomalies in the composition, especially in the figures on the right wall, where the laurel bushes are inserted more as fillings than as rhythmic separating elements, the heaviness of the drapery, the rough delineations of faces seen in profile, the use of violent and discordant color, the slovenly outline (redeemed to some extent by a certain boldness and spontaneousness in the treatment and construction of the figures), all give the impression of a popular style of painting.

There are, however, suggestions that the painter was capable of better things, especially when he is dealing with traditional themes (as in the decorative elements of the pendentives) or copying compositions and figures of a static, decorative order, as in the triclinium scene and in the procession of musicians and attendants on the left wall. The drawing of some of the heads (that of the lyre-player, for instance, on the right wall) shows a purity of line, an evident power of expression, a mature understanding of the new stylistic orientations of the extreme phase of the severe style (e.g. in the practically profile eyes), which strike a definite contrast with the awkward insipidity of the other figures. This is another token of the general discontinuity and uncertainty of style prevailing in the painted decoration of this tomb.

DANCING WOMAN AND LYRE-PLAYER. TOMB OF THE TRICLINIUM, TARQUINII.

TOMB OF THE TRICLINIUM

The decorations of the Tomb of the Triclinium (dated ca. 470 B.C.) have been preserved from destruction by the difficult and delicate process of detaching them from the wall on which they were painted and they are now to be seen in the Museum of Tarquinia. Despite the ravages of time, the high quality of this picture cycle, one of the noblest that has come down to us from antiquity, makes itself unequivocally felt. The subjects are arranged on the walls in much the same way as those in the Tomb of the Leopards : the banquet on the back wall and music and dancing on either side. When we compare these pictures with those on similar themes in other tombs, we cannot but be struck by the artist's personal genius and the exquisite refinement of his work.

A youth playing the double pipes is walking with dancing steps among the flowering bushes of a garden, towards his masters' table. He has the short curly black hair then in fashion. The stalwart yet supple body, painted in reddish-brown, is clad in a white transparent chlamys, edged with rows of dots; slipping down from his shoulders along his arms, it reveals his torso. He is wearing brown shoes. The side-view position has been cleverly rendered by an adroit foreshortening of the shoulders, chest and arms; the eye, however, is still ingenuously drawn front-view, though the face is shown in profile, the pupil is placed well forward and the man is gazing vaguely upwards as if lost in a day-dream. The slim, slightly curved and extremely sensitive fingers of the right hand are sliding along the pipe. He is flanked by a shrub with large blue bell-shaped flowers and by a laurel bush; five birds perched on twigs form a circle round the pipe-player as though spellbound by the shrill, insistent melody.

The artist has pictured a dream figure in the landscape of a dream. The peculiar charm of this picture consists above all in the elegant simplicity of its supple linework together with the delicacy of the colors which ring the changes on transitions from white and pinkish white to red-brown, brown and black. This combination of a smoothly flowing, continuous line with soft, unemphatic colors admirably conveys the impression of a gentle, dreamy youth; we might almost say that we have here the transposition of a musical effect on to the pictorial plane—not only by reason of the picture's subject matter, but also and above all owing to the artist's handling of forms.

Here there is nothing of that isolation to which the purely descriptive and narrative themes of archaism relegated the human figure; far otherwise, this young man seems to be listening both to an inner voice and to the voices of the outside world, at one with the harmonious order of men and things. Conveyed with a fine sobriety, the landscape elements are still conditioned by a balanced schematic decorative pattern of ancient origin (the alternation of small trees and human figures). They, too, seem to be imbued with the same inner life, the same musical conception as is implicit in the figure of the young dancing pipe-player. Indeed plants, flowers and birds fall into place quite naturally in the compositional scheme. The choice of motifs, the dynamic energy of the living elements, the exquisite *finesse* of both drawing and color, vouch for an inventive and refined maturity only to be found in great art periods and in the highest cultures known to history.

This depiction of the musician, framed between the vertical stems of the flowering shrubs, might form a picture complete in itself; indeed there are indications on the plaster that the picture sequence was planned in separate compartments, demarcated by the stems. But we should not overlook the fact that this figure forms part of a long frieze comprising many similar subjects. And though each figure differs from the others, all are caught up in the same ideal rhythm, share in the same emotion and the same stylistic inspiration. Here, transcending the conventions of time-honored patterns and decorative formulas, the artist envisaged an underlying correspondence between his isolated scenes. Never before had an Etruscan artist achieved this very real and all-pervasive unity in a large-scale decoration.

PIPE-PLAYER AND BIRDS. TOMB OF THE TRICLINIUM, TARQUINII.

MALE DANCER. TOMB OF THE TRICLINIUM, TARQUINII.

WOMAN DANCING. TOMB OF THE TRICLINIUM, TARQUINII.

MALE DANCER. TOMB OF THE TRICLINIUM, TARQUINII.

Our appraisal of the stylistic qualities of the paintings in the Tomb of the Triclinium must be chiefly based on the figures on the side walls, that is to say the frieze with scenes of music and dancing. The banqueting scene on the back wall has gone to pieces, though not to the extent of preventing us from forming an opinion of it, especially as regards the general nature of the composition. The thematic lay-out resembles that of the Tomb of the Leopards; we see couples reclining on couches (the women and men alike are black-haired), surrounded by attendants, while under the couches domestic animals can be seen, waiting presumably to pick up the scraps that their masters let fall. The composition is formal, dignified, and there is a skillful interplay of verticals and horizontals: the legs of the couches, the figures and the hanging chaplets being balanced by the horizontal lines of the triclinium. Though the attitudes of the figures, the slightly bent heads and the elegantly languid movements of the arms are deliberately sedate (in keeping with the dignity of the august owners of the tomb), stylistically they show analogies with the treatment of the dancers and musicians on the side walls. These dancers are spaced out, youths and girls alternating, between foliage with a single musician (also dancing) posted at the end of each row, to 'set the measures of dance; the pipe-player already described figures on the right, and a lyre-player on the the left. The entrance is flanked, right and left, by horsemen.

Such is the artistic quality of the paintings in the Tomb of the Triclinium that the essentially decorative elements, as well as the painted friezes, are well worth studying. As in the Tomb of the Chariots, human figures are included in the scene figuring on the pediment, this being necessitated by the traditional, symmetrical lay-out of such decorations. Noteworthy, however, is the use of a design of ivy-leaves and berries, sprouting from a big stem and making a very striking decorative pattern. Particularly effective are the chromatic alternations of white, browns and greens. These motifs extend to the spiral pilaster of the pediment and spread across the flat surface of the central bay of the ceiling; the raking cornice on the other hand has a checkered pattern of squares in the same three colors, while a band of ivy-leaves runs along the top of the walls, over the historiated frieze.

The execution of these paintings vouches for the artist's mastery of the technical procedures developed during the previous decade. We do not find any preparatory incised lines (except for partitioning off the various scenes)—which suggests that the artist worked from a preliminary sketch; this, indeed, is confirmed by the over-all unity and balance of the composition and by the perfection of the details. So as to reduce the figures to the right proportions without losing any of the harmony of the original design, cartoons or templates may have been employed. Both the red-brown or black outlines, and the interior descriptive lines are drawn with wonderful regularity and fineness, the latter being invisible to the naked eye in the passages of dark color (e. g. in the flesh tints of the male figures and in the hair). The traditional method of painting each circumscribed area in flat even color is modified in some places (the hair, the bodies of the birds) by touches of blended color, and sometimes even by scumbles which clearly indicate attempts to render chiaroscuro effects (for example in the women's arms).

In the decoration of this tomb we find an harmonious unity of composition, style and technique that shows it to be the work of an artist with a strong, well-developed personality. Rarely, indeed, among the unknown painters of the tombs of Tarquinii, does the study and appraisal of an individual artist present so much interest and offer so much scope as in this Tomb of the Triclinium. The problem can be approached from two angles: from that of the cultural formation of the painter and from that of his idiosyncrasies, his obvious imaginative genius and his power, and his technical procedures. In a general way the art of the painter of the Tomb of the Triclinium derives from a school sponsored by certain Attic vase-painters belonging to the last phase of the severe style; for example, by the Painter of Kleophrades, the Painter of Brygos, the Painter of Telephos. Their works obviously pertain to a type of painting that flourished in Greece, and notably in Athens, at the time of the Persian Wars and during the years immediately following. But neither do these chronological *data* nor the conditions of his environment suffice to account for the cultural make-up of the painter of the Tomb of the Triclinium. In some respects he seems to keep to methods of an earlier age, deriving perhaps from a local tradition—as in the stylized beak-shaped folds of the drapery, and the conventional rendering of the edges of the tunics, with their points turned upwards so as to express movement. On the other hand, the contemplative attitude of some of the figures, the fluent rendering of some heads, and especially the tentative hints of chiaroscuro, may seem to foreshadow the ideological and formal innovations of classical art, and can even be assimilated to the procedures of certain Attic vase-painters of the transitional phase (for example, the Painter of Pistoxenos).

Thus we have in the painter of the Triclinium an artist of a wide, refined and up-to-date aesthetic culture; possibly he may have been a Greek artist who settled in Etruria and adapted himself to local requirements. It would however be more plausible to see in him an Etruscan artist, well versed in the traditions of tomb painting at Tarquinii, but none the less in touch with contemporary art movements. Moreover he displays a far-ranging imaginative power which makes itself felt both in the conception and in the execution of his figures. In fact the characteristics already noticed in the pipe-player reappear, in a more or less pronounced manner, in the other dancers. In the case of some of them, and especially in the female figures, the freely flowing line acquires a sort of gyratory movement harmonized to that of the dance, which sometimes seems arrested in a sudden languor and sometimes, when all the heads bend forward or are tossed back, expresses a voluptuous abandon. The postures of the bodies, the steps and gestures, the fluttering draperies—all are pervaded by a dynamic rhythm, which makes this picture one of the most effective and most elegant works of all ancient art.

True, the depiction of movement and emotion was nothing new in late archaic Greek painting. The originality of the painter of the Tomb of the Triclinium consists above all in his having handled such themes on purely personal lines, and with a unique emotive drive. Here, for the first time in funerary decoration, we find tokens of subtle, all-pervasive, warmly human feeling, in striking contrast with the primitive, ruthless realism of the older tombs.

BANQUET SCENE. TOMB OF THE FUNERAL COUCH, TARQUINII.

TOMB OF THE FUNERAL COUCH

If, as some authorities believe, it were true that in the decoration of this tomb we have another instance of work done by the artist who painted the Tomb of the Triclinium, we should be in the fortunate and unique position of being able to study the achievements of one and the same artist in two practically intact groups of pictures, both of high stylistic quality. That there is a real kinship between the decorations of the two tombs is evidenced by the striking resemblances in the general conception and the drawing of the figures. The Tomb of the Funeral Couch is certainly the later: probably it was painted round about 460 B.C., for traces of the influence of early classical drawing are clearly apparent.

The rather damaged decoration of the Tomb of the Funeral Couch is noteworthy for the special nature of its theme. The murals of the back wall extend beyond the upper edge of the band of the frieze and occupy the whole frontage, thus comprising a single monumental composition which thereafter is prolonged on to the frieze of the side walls. The scene is presented as taking place in a large pavilion hung with a curtain, upheld by poles bedecked with foliage, and open in front; the sides of the pavilion extend so as to overlap part of the side walls. Beneath it, plumb in the center, on the back wall, stands a huge couch adorned with heavy embroidered coverlets, on which are placed, towards the right, two groups of identical objects, each set out in the following order: a white cone with spiral stripes and a wreath of leaves at the bottom, lying on two cushions, to the left of which is a cloak overlapping the edge of the coverlet. On either side of this bulky dais are human figures: on the right, banqueters reclining in the foreground, and youths standing behind them with their arms raised towards the couch as a sign of salute and homage; on the left only one female figure remains, also turned towards the couch with both arms raised; further back is a table bearing a large *crater* decorated with light figures on a dark ground. The scene of the banquet is prolonged on the side walls until it reaches the end of the pavilion. Beyond this the usual scenes of music, dancing and games are closely aligned in an unbroken sequence.

Many attempts have been made to interpret this unique and somewhat obscure composition. However the most likely explanation would seem to be that it has funerary associations. The banquet, music, dancing and athletic contests belong to the usual repertory of the paintings of archaic Etruscan tombs, and are closely connected with the funeral rites. The homage paid to the great couch which dominates the scene, in the center of these manifestations, recalls the homage paid to the painted door of the Tomb of the Augurs, to the *crater* in the Tomb of the Lionesses and to the sepulchral niche of the Tomba della Pulcella (this last, however, belongs to the fifth century and is later than the Tomb of the Funeral Couch). It should also be noted that the curious symbolic objects arranged one on top of the other on the couch are placed on the right, where would be the heads of the deceased reclining on the festal couches. Here we therefore probably have the depiction of a precise moment of the obsequies, with the catafalque on which the dead man was laid and where his insignia were placed. In this painting, however, the last honors are being paid to two dead people, who may be identified as a married couple of the family for whom the tomb was decorated. If this be the correct explanation, conclusions can be drawn that are also of interest for evaluating the creative genius of the artist. He may be regarded as the first to give an over-all, fully integrated depiction of a funeral scene, without regard to the traditional fragmentary character assumed by archaic painting with a view to picturing this or that separate aspect of the ceremonies in compositions divided up in accordance with a pre-established rhythm. These attempts to effect a visual synthesis and psychological unity vouch for tendencies running parallel to the classic ideals. This is also seen in some of the separate groups of the figures, such as in that extraordinary detail of two youths holding a racehorse which they are about to harness to a chariot.

RACEHORSE HELD BY YOUTHS. TOMB OF THE FUNERAL COUCH, TARQUINII.

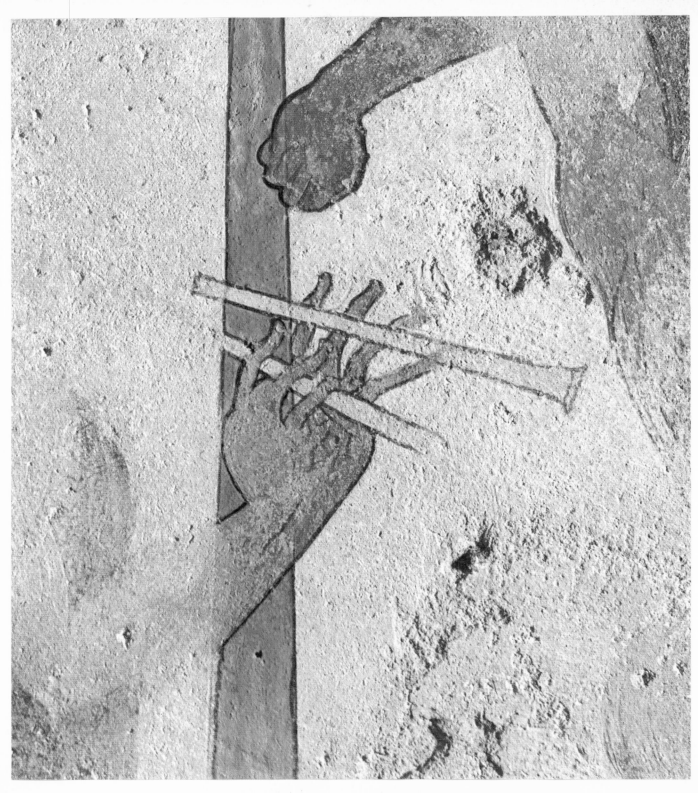

PIPE-PLAYER'S HAND, DETAIL. TOMB OF THE FUNERAL COUCH, TARQUINII.

The painting in the Tomb of the Funeral Couch, as far as its superficial aspects are concerned, still belongs to the art of extreme archaism, as is apparent in the frontal position of the eyes, the geometric folds of the drapery, and so forth. But it is also clear that Greek classical influence is beginning to make itself felt, if only in a rudimentary way, not only in the artist's over-all conception of the composition and in the formal characteristics shared by these frescos with those of the Tomb of the Triclinium (soft modeling, flowing outlines), but also in certain specific procedures, such as the placing of the figures in two rows, with the front ones partially hiding the back ones (this particular device is said to stem from the painting of Polygnotos).

However, inherited elements and external influences play only a limited part in the quite special stylistic inventions which can be seen in the few figures of the tomb which, despite the damaged color, can be clearly perceived and evaluated. They have

ARM OF A BANQUETER, DETAIL. TOMB OF THE FUNERAL COUCH, TARQUINII.

much of that particular charm which is found in many of the Greek figure-paintings of the transitional period between archaism and classicism and in those of the incipient classical phase (a charm which renewed itself many centuries later in the Italian art of the fifteenth century). It might indeed be said that with the paintings of the Tomb of the Funeral Couch even Etruscan art took a classical turn—which most regrettably had no issue.

In the fragment already mentioned showing youths holding back a horse, the finely balanced tautness of the composition is in keeping with the fluent, elegant drawing of the figures. In the youth with bent head behind the horse, the vertical lines of the body and the correspondingly oblique lines of the left arm and of the left leg, extended in the effort of controlling the restless animal, form a tense, taut whole. The movement of unavailing restiveness on the part of the thin, nervous horse gives evidence of quick sketching. Nor does the non-naturalistic, conventional blue coloring (partly vanished) clash with the expressive lifelikeness of the drawing; it is indeed a vital element of the sophisticated abstractionism that sets the tone of the whole painting.

But the exquisite art of the painter of the Tomb of the Funeral Couch is apparent above all in the details: in the expressive hands of the youth playing the double pipes on the right wall, his tapering fingers dancing along his instrument to the rhythm of the melody. We see it also in the arm of one of the feasters on the back wall telling out against the blue background of a mantle, as he holds forth a drink-offering.

In some of the delicate touches of the drawing and coloring, in the pensive serenity of the figures, in the harmony and indeed musical quality of the composition, are characteristics that appear also in the Tomb of the Triclinium, to which, for that matter, this painting as a whole is closely related as regards the color technique and ornamentation of the ceiling (the free use of graffito preparation in the drawing of the figures is, however, a distinctive element). Nevertheless the frescos in the Tomb of the Funeral Couch seem to reflect a more tranquil vision and a still greater sense of meditative calm—owing perhaps to the different nature of the subject. The way in which the unconstraint shown in the rendering of movement and the analytic, rhythmical, almost matter-of-fact depiction of the Triclinium are set off against the firmly knit structure of the scenes and groups, is a sign of a maturer art. It would be difficult to find a definite answer to the problems raised by these resemblances and differences. The family likeness between the two series of paintings can certainly not be attributed only to similarities of time and ' climate,' considering the chronological discrepancy that probably exists between them, and taking into account the fact that some contemporary monuments have a resonance and quality completely different. Possibly the decorator of the Tomb of the Funeral Couch was a pupil of the painter of the Tomb of the Triclinium. Or why not risk the yet more attractive hypothesis that both tombs were painted by the same master at different stages of his development ?

BACK WALL, DETAIL. FRANCESCA GIUSTINIANI TOMB, TARQUINII.

GIUSTINIANI TOMB

As against the glorious *ensembles* created by the painters of such tombs as that of the Triclinium and the Funeral Couch, we find less pretentious works, even trade products, that reiterate the formulas and ideas of the severe style of painting, right through the fifth century. The Francesca Giustiniani, Querciola and Pulcella tombs can be numbered amongst these. In spite of the archaic or sub-archaic features of their style, they certainly belong already to the period when classic art had triumphed in the Greek world. It is, however, rather difficult to fix a precise date for them. Somewhere about the middle of the century might be suggested for the Francesca Giustiniani Tomb, though without excluding the possibility of an even more recent date.

The lay-out of the decoration is the traditional one of the archaic tombs of Tarquinii. The slopes of the ceiling are painted with red transversal bands imitating beams. The pediment shows two leopards flanking the usual pilaster. The frieze on the walls (of which little, except the bottom part, can be seen) contains scenes of music and dancing and perhaps athletic contests, and is a rather confused and inharmonious composition. A couple are portrayed on the right-hand side of the back wall : the man in a richly bordered blue cloak is walking towards the left with his right arm raised, perhaps as a gesture of salute, and holding a small crook in his left hand; the woman, who is turning towards him with one arm by her side and the other raised, is sumptuously, almost cumbrously dressed in a long orange-red chiton with crosses and dots embroidered in red, above which she wears a thicker red jacket; she is also wearing a necklace, armlets and a diadem. Another woman follows, also elaborately dressed but with no diadem on her short hair (we may assume she is a servant), and is playing the double pipe. A chariot with its driver figures at the end. Another chariot can just be made out amongst the practically indistinguishable figures on the other walls. The noble couple at the back are most likely the owners of the tomb, or the deceased. It is highly doubtful if the artist has depicted them in the act of dancing. More likely the man is saluting his lady before stepping into the chariot. This chariot, if it has to do with the journey into the next world, would thus be the first introduction of a fantastic motif into the repertory of realistic subjects. But it is also possible that the chariots are indicative of the usual funeral games.

The structure of the figures and the treatment of the drapery still substantially adhere to the formulas of the severe style, though signs of a more advanced artistic training, including the plastic and perspective effects of classical design, appear here and there. But these paintings are a far cry indeed from the fine traditions of Etruscan painting of the severe style, as expressed in frescos such as those in the Tombs of the Triclinium and the Funeral Couch, and show little understanding of contemporary Greek art. Thus the paintings of the Francesca Giustiniani Tomb confirm the existence of productions of a lower order—one which must also be taken into account if we are to get a complete picture of the figure-painting of Tarquinii during the fifth century. They at once reflect the then prevailing procedures of monumental art, and at the same time re-echo and cling with incredible tenacity to motifs belonging to much more ancient times. While this interpretation of contemporary artistic developments is extremely brilliant, it is also, in many respects, somewhat obtuse and vulgar. There is no real life in the drawing of the figures, and the variety of gestures and the wealth of decorative details do not suffice to conceal the poverty of the inspiration. The technique is second-rate, even coarse.

Yet there are also piquant touches. Thus, despite the slovenly drawing, the detail of the head of one of the two chariot horses, painted on the back wall, has the charm of an ingenious improvisation, thanks to the vigorous ' folk-art ' rendering of the large muzzle and the two small divergent ears. Moreover, this detail is given a peculiar, fabulous life of its own by violent contrasts of fantastic color: elements inherited

HORSES' HEADS. FRANCESCA GIUSTINIANI TOMB, TARQUINII.

from archaism, but which here do not seem to have any real connection with the delightful ingenuousness of more ancient figures. The paler blue profile, behind the red one, might almost be a shadow.

Extant works of art of the fifth century B.C., such as the decoration of the Francesca Giustiniani Tomb, show that during the course of the century a steadily increasing disparity was making itself felt in Etruscan painting between the productions of superior style and technique and trade products. This phenomenon was not so much in evidence in more ancient painting. On the other hand it became characteristic in the output of the Hellenistic period. This process tallies with the industrialization of funerary and votive sculpture which also began in the fifth century. In the case of painting, the appearance of works that are obviously second-rate so far as conception, style and technique are concerned, alongside products of better quality, might on the one hand be attributed to the decadence of the schools of craftsmen, but also perhaps to the then prevailing economic crisis which must have obliged customers to content themselves with the work of second-rank artists or even of simple artisans. To this same cause, in an aggravated form, may be attributed the slackening off and indeed (at least as far as we can judge) temporary cessation of the production of works of art between the end of the fifth century and the first half of the fourth.

3

CLASSICAL INFLUENCES

(FOURTH CENTURY B.C.)

As we have already observed, there was a definite break between the archaic Etruscan paintings and the monuments of the Hellenistic period, and this synchronized with a period of decadence in the cities of Etruria preceding their conquest by the Romans. During this phase, the gradual extinction of the local art traditions kept pace with the emergence in Etruria of classical motifs, especially of those of the great Attic art of the second half of the fifth and of the fourth century, imported directly from the cultural centers of Magna Graecia.

It must, however, be noted that the Etruscan world, fundamentally alien as it was to the spiritual problems and poetic aspirations of Hellenistic classicism, took over its themes and procedures in a quite detached manner; that is to say it treated them as pleasantly ornamental devices suitable for the embellishment of buildings or objects. Mythological compositions of Greek origin were faithfully copied, even though subjects belonging to the Etruscan iconography and elements of the indigenous tradition were sometimes grafted on to them. This choice of subjects is seen chiefly in minor artifacts such as painted pottery (sometimes polychrome) and drawings engraved on mirrors and cists.

Generally speaking the large-scale painting in houses and temples derived from the same imitative and decorative tendencies. We see instances of this also in the paintings of the sarcophagi. As regards the tomb paintings to be seen at Tarquinii and around Orvieto, the problem seems more complex. The choice of themes was directed by religious requirements and these themes had to relate to the world of the dead. Thus the imitation of mythological scenes taken from classical art was subordinated to a specific purpose—of conjuring up the underworld and its denizens by representations similar to those of the Greek Hades, but permeated with an atmosphere of fantasy and often of terror, in accord with the indigenous beliefs. In these scenes the artists combined typically Greek elements with realistic details recalling the ancient local traditions as well as certain new creations of Etruscan inspiration (especially in portraying the very characteristic, sometimes quite horrific demons of the Etruscan Hades). The stylistic and technical quality of these paintings is often rather poor; though they are not without expressive touches of marked originality. Thus both the compositional program and the cultural background of the decorators are illustrated in the composite inspiration of these paintings.

AMAZONS ATTACKING A GREEK. SARCOPHAGUS FROM TARQUINII. ARCHAEOLOGICAL MUSEUM, FLORENCE.

SARCOPHAGUS OF THE AMAZONS

Etruscan sarcophagi (sarcophagi were more frequently used from the fifth century B.C. onwards) are generally decorated in bas-relief, usually polychrome. Sarcophagi with paintings on the cases are, so far as we know, extremely rare. Of these the Sarcophagus of the Amazons, found in a tomb at Tarquinii and now in the Archaeological Museum, Florence, is the only one that is fairly well preserved. It has a roof-shaped lid, with rough sculpture depicting Actaeon devoured by his dogs in the frontal spaces. Painted on all four sides with scenes of Battles of Amazons, with pilasters at the corners and a cyma at the bottom, the case itself is obviously of more ancient origin than the lid. The funerary inscription of a deceased woman named Ramtha Huzcnai, now inscribed on the lid, has been clumsily scratched with a metal point on the front of the case, disfiguring the painted surface.

On one of the long sides of the sarcophagus, two four-horsed chariots are painted with Amazons pressing forward to attack Greek warriors who are fighting on foot. The left-hand chariot is rendered in foreshortening. One of the Amazons in the chariot is launching a spear, while the other leans forward, intent on driving the four mettlesome white horses. A Greek warrior in glistening armor has fallen in front of the horses' hoofs. In this composition the handling of perspective and strongly plastic forms in rapid movement, the play of light and shade, and the harmony of the arrangement and colors illustrate the lay-out and technique of classical art in its maturity. Particularly noteworthy is the sense of volume conveyed by the horses' bodies bound by firm flowing outlines; this is obtained by the use of grey shading, implemented here and there by strokes, simple or crossed. Patches of intenser color emphasize the perspective of the body of the chariot, painted in red, and of the yellow wheels, and the blue iron tires. Similar methods are employed in the rendering of the nude parts of the male figures painted in red-brown, and of the women's in pink, the red-brown hair, the drapery, the harness and the arms. There is also a vague suggestion of a rocky landscape. The background seems originally to have been blue, but only a few traces remain.

AMAZONS DRIVING A QUADRIGA. SARCOPHAGUS FROM TARQUINII.
ARCHAEOLOGICAL MUSEUM, FLORENCE.

BATTLE OF GREEKS AND AMAZONS. SARCOPHAGUS FROM TARQUINII.
ARCHAEOLOGICAL MUSEUM, FLORENCE.

The paintings of the Sarcophagus of the Amazons have a quite exceptional documentary value in the series of examples of pictorial art that have been brought to light in the Etruscan territory. Even when the particular character of this monument is taken into account (as against the mural decorations existing in the tombs)—since we are here concerned both with special proportions and a special kind of painting, on highly polished calcareous stone—there still remain technical and stylistic elements which distinguish this frieze from the other paintings and give it an aspect of particular refinement. Here we obviously have a work which, although pertaining to an unpretentious class of art, of a decorative, funerary and private order, attains the standard of the finest painting of the Graeco-Italic world during the classical period. This is all the more remarkable since actually at this time Etruscan funerary painting was passing through a decadent phase and the examples of it that have come down to us are of slight or relatively secondary value.

We have already seen how the technical qualities of his craftsmanship—which has sometimes the delicacy of the miniature—enable the classical artist to realize that relatively objective vision in the arrangement and construction of the figures which is one of the outstanding aspects of the pictorial art of classicism. The competent handling of perspective, the freedom with which the figures move in space, the impression of plastic relief, all appear here as problems that have already been solved thanks to mature experience, by means of line and chiaroscuro. The colors function in strict conjunction with the descriptive realism. Subtle modulations and skillful blendings implement an extremely varied range of half-tones derived from the five basic hues: white, black, yellow, red and blue.

The spirit of classical art is however also and above all manifest in the arrangement of the composition and the finely rhythmical grouping of the figures. Thus on one of the long sides we see a group of Amazons fighting against the Greeks placed in the center, and symmetrically disposed on either side are two-figure groups of a Greek striking a fallen Amazon and a Greek fighting a mounted Amazon. On the other side are the two groups of Amazons' quadrigae, each in conflict with two Greeks. The short sides show a Greek with two Amazons, in different attitudes.

It is obvious that this frieze copies or imitates one of those well-known compositions of Battles of Amazons which were so widely diffused in Greek monumental painting and sculpture of the classical period, starting from the famous works of Polygnotos and Mikon. However, except for some incidental iconographic parallels with Greek monuments, it is difficult to specify the exact prototype of this composition. It can only be said that it must certainly have belonged to the painting of the sixth century, in view of the intent, emotive expression of the faces and unmistakable affinities of composition notably with the Greek sarcophagus with reliefs depicting Battles of Amazons in the Museum of Vienna.

Was the painter who decorated the Tarquinian sarcophagus a Greek or an Etruscan? There are certainly iconographic details (such as the Amazons fighting from their chariots) and elements of dress which are not found in depictions of Battles of Amazons in the area of Greece proper: e.g. in reliefs, vase-paintings and the like. On the other hand several of these appear in the compositions of the painted vases of Southern Italy; moreover, a certain family likeness, also from the point of view of the style, seems to connect the painting of this sarcophagus with the designs of the so-called Apulian vases made at Tarentum. It may, therefore, not seem too far-fetched to suppose that the case of this sarcophagus was decorated by a Greek painter of Southern Italy working in Etruria, or by an Etruscan pupil of his, towards the middle of the fourth century.

PREPARATIONS FOR THE BANQUET, DETAIL. GOLINI TOMB, ORVIETO.

GOLINI TOMB

The much damaged paintings in the two tombs of Porano, near Orvieto, were recently removed from the walls and are now preserved in the Archaeological Museum at Florence. The largest of them depicted banqueting scenes in the Other World, with dead members of the Lecate and Leinie families taking part in them, in the presence of Hades and Persephone. Of particular interest are the realistic depictions of the preparations for the feast; we are shown servants and cooks going about their tasks exactly as in life. The influence of classical art is evident in the painter's racy, vivacious treatment of these scenes and also in the way they are presented; none the less the background atmosphere is quite definitely Etruscan. This work belongs to the last quarter of the fourth century B.C.

PREPARATIONS FOR THE BANQUET, DETAIL. GOLINI TOMB, ORVIETO.

THE TOMB OF ORCUS

EARLIER CHAMBER

The sepulchre or, rather, pair of sepulchres known as the Tomb of Orcus (or Polyphemus) is of exceptional interest in view of the light which it throws on the evolution of Tarquinian painting. For we have here two distinct tombs built at quite different periods and subsequently connected by a passage-way between them. Thus they supply illustrations of three successive phases of Etruscan art: in the earlier tomb, in the second and later tomb and finally in the connecting passage, which contains a single picture. Unfortunately all these paintings have been seriously damaged not only by retouchings but by the vandalism of modern researchers who have tried to detach portions of the painted surface from the walls.

The older chamber, a very large one, has a ceiling sloping down on either side, a central pilaster, inclined walls, and ledges for the sarcophagi. As in the Orvieto tomb the frieze depicts banquets in the Underworld, the names of the persons taking part being recorded in inscriptions. This frieze is almost completely destroyed and in view of the exceptionally high quality of the painting in it this is a loss we must bitterly deplore. All that survives is a fragment spanning the angle formed by the back wall and the right-hand wall. On the latter the banqueting couch was painted, with a man and a woman reclining together. Only a small part of the woman's head remains. On the adjoining part of the back wall is a complete figure, that of a huge winged demon moving towards the left. Further on there are traces of another banqueting scene, showing men reclining on couches with servants waiting on them, in a setting of small trees. Throughout its length the frieze is bordered, above, by a decorative band of leaves in various colors, and, below, by a line of stylized waves.

Members of the Tarquinian aristocracy were buried here, persons of very high rank, judging by the inscriptions. They belonged to several, most likely inter-related, families and it would seem that this tomb had been in long use before the passage-way was built linking it to the near-by sepulchral chamber. We may probably assign its original building and painting to the last decades of the fourth century B.C., that is to say to the period when Tarquinii was gradually coming under Roman domination. The enlargement of the sepulchre (it was most probably in the course of this operation that the frescos on the left wall were destroyed) would seem to have taken place about two centuries later.

The fragment consisting of the woman's head is rightly considered as one of the most interesting " anthology pieces " not only of Etruscan but of all ancient art.

It is located on the right wall of the tomb and shows a lady beside her husband, Arnth Velcha; the inscription tells us that her name is Velia (the family name has been destroyed). She is reclining on the banqueting couch according to the custom illustrated in the most ancient tombs, and not seated as in pictures of the Hellenistic epoch. Behind her shoulders looms up a weirdly shaped black, or rather greenish-black, cloud ; it has wavy, straggling contours and occupies part of the wall surface on which the head is painted, serving as its background. As in the Orvieto pictures, this is an ingenious device of the painter's for conveying to us that the banqueting scene is placed in the netherworld of the Shades.

The lady is wearing a light-hued tunic and a wrap of the same color, with a broad scalloped trimming round the collar. Her hair is bunched up on the back of her head and held in place by a light-colored ribbon. In front her curls hang loosely down her cheeks in accordance with a fashion followed by both Greek and Italian ladies in the fourth century. On her head is a diadem of myrtle and olive leaves, and she is wearing a considerable quantity of jewelry: large earrings shaped like bunches of grapes and two necklaces, a short one with small round beads and a longer one with round and cylindrical beads. The gold of these ornaments has the same reddish-brown hue as Velia's hair.

The outline of her face is firmly drawn, both its profile and its interior details being clearly indicated. While here and there it is adumbrated by the preliminary incised contour-line, it is also delicately traced in black. Nevertheless the telling contrasts between the bright passages of the face, neck and drapery and the dark death-cloud rising in the background, and those between the dark hair and the pale wall surface above the cloud, tend to supplant the contour-line and make us see the clearness of the profile as resulting, rather, from a juxtaposition of contrasting planes of color, a subtly planned and delicate chromatic effect. On the other hand, for the leaves of the garland, the jewels and the folds of the drapery the artist has depended more obviously on linework. Generally speaking he shows a certain timidity in the use of chiaroscuro, though he employs it to good effect in certain details of the face, noteworthy being the soft nuances of reddish-brown shadowing the nose, cheek, and eyelids. Color modulations and shaded passages can be seen in the handling of the hair and the jewelry, in which (in the earring and the small necklace) there is an almost impressionist dis-agregation of form. But however much we may admire the artist's craftsmanship and technical procedures, the appeal of this picture is due far more to the exquisitely rendered profile. The broad curve of the eye with its big, mournful iris tells out against the smooth, slightly indented line of the forehead and nose, while between the full, pale-pink, half-parted lips the dark recession of the drooping mouth makes a deep cleft. Velia, one would think, is day-dreaming. Profiles of this kind, with the same stylization of eyes, nose and lips, are to be found in the delicately drawn faces on fourth-century Attic vases. But it is only in this painting in the Tomb of Orcus that we sense the grandeur of this exquisite creation of classical art in its most fully evolved form; indeed we have here a work of the very highest quality both technically and stylistically. The Etruscan painter who made the portrait of this beautiful dead woman clearly took for his models the noblest extant forms of graphic art and interpreted them with intelligence and flawless taste.

In attempting to fix the precise chronology of the oldest picture sequence in the Tomb of Orcus we come up against the same difficulty as in the Golini Tomb at Orvieto. For comparisons with the contemporary developments of Greek drawing seem much

WOMAN'S HEAD. TOMB OF ORCUS, TARQUINII.

too limited and vague to provide any reliable basis for dating. However, in the striking iconographical affinity between the head of Velia and analogous types to be found in fourth-century Attic pottery, and the artist's sensitive feeling for the classical line in all its purity and harmony, as well as in certain extraneous indications, we have perhaps enough to justify the assumption that these paintings antedate—if only by a short time—the beginning of the Hellenistic period properly so called; that is to say they were painted towards the close of the fourth century, and are thus more or less contemporary with the Orvieto paintings.

Yet the picture we are given here of the Netherworld differs somewhat from that at Orvieto, and in this work the Etruscans made a step forward in adapting the Greek Hades to their own beliefs and creative idiosyncrasies. Here, for the first time in tomb painting we are shown one of the hair-raising demons which in Etruscan art of the Hellenistic period appear again and again in such a variety of fanciful forms. These monsters constitute a lurid transformation of the type of male spirits peopling Hell which had already appeared several times in Etruria, and which, moreover, were not unknown to Greek art. They were made by grafting animal characteristics on to human figures and painting the flesh-parts in weird bluish or greenish colors, a practice that has been interpreted as an attempt to depict putrefying flesh. However, in Pausanias (*Periegesis*, X, 28, 7 sq.) we find a description of Eurynomos, a blue-bodied demon of death, as painted by the great Polygnotos in his picture of the Underworld in the Cnidian Lesche at Delphi; thus Greek classical art may very possibly have provided the Etruscans with prototypes of these infernal beings.

But whereas Greek artists as a rule avoided this night side of things, the Etruscans developed it with considerable gusto. In the oldest chamber of the Tomb of Orcus the type of Charun is already well defined (this was the local interpretation of the Greek Charon, symbol and divinity of death, ferryman of the dead across the Styx). He is represented wearing a short, belted tunic, with two crossed thongs upon his breast, and high boots. His face is human except for his nose, shaped like the beak of a bird of prey, and his hair, which is a tangled mass of snakes; he has two huge wings and his flesh is green. Beside his head rises a big, crested snake. This merciless, death-dealing god is gripping a rod, presumably the handle of the hammer symbolizing his function.

4

THE PAINTING OF THE HELLENISTIC PERIOD

(THIRD-FIRST CENTURY B.C.)

At the time of the Roman conquest and the pacification of central Italy, the Etruscan cities seem to have enjoyed a general cultural revival, which manifested itself in their art. But on the whole the art production of this period reveals a diversity of inspirations, a dramatic accentuation of conflicting tendencies and a discontinuity in stylistic values which can only be explained as the outcome of a cultural predicament. It would seem that we have here a period of transition from the ancient local procedures of the Italic peoples to the more generalized inspirations of Hellenism and Rome.

That this cultural predicament made itself felt in painting is evidenced by the tombs of Tarquinii, Caere, Vulci. (Some other monuments of great importance, now unfortunately lost, are known only from descriptions or all too often unsatisfactory reproductions.) The influence of Greek art is still present, and revealed in the assimilation of classical models and in the gradual infiltration of motifs stemming from the various art centers of the Hellenistic world. Compositions and figure types are more or less faithfully imitated, while the artists' execution keeps pace with the general advance of pictorial technique. However the persistence or re-emergence of indigenous traditional elements is also noticeable, though as a rule these are no more than incidental " tricks of the trade." The decoration of tombs was now debased to the level of vulgar popular productions. On the other hand a sometimes almost feverish quest of new means of expression, suitable to the deep spiritual message that the subject matter of these pictures is intended to convey, often makes its presence felt.

Indeed, in Etruscan funerary painting of the Hellenistic period, we find spiritual motifs canalizing the efforts of the decorators in a uniform direction, whatever their education, temperament or cultural level. That agonizing problem of the after-life now becomes the leading theme of the subjects represented, and manifests itself in pictures that continue to move away from the classical notions of the other world and align themselves with the tangled, mysterious beliefs of the Etruscans. (Scenes of the torments and wanderings of the soul were for the most part represented at Tarqui-nii, in paintings which are now lost or have gone to pieces, such as those of the Tartaglia Tomb and the Tomb of the Cardinal.)

But the theme of death is not handled in any abstract manner. It is linked up with ancestor worship, and thus with an exaltation of the racial pride which lingered on in the decadent Etruscan nobility. So much so that realistic portrayals of deceased noblemen came to predominate in these pictures; indeed they became the leitmotiv of this art. This desire for commemoration of the dead manifested itself in a tendency towards the individual, expressive portrait—in which we have one of the most significant and vital manifestations of the Etruscan art of this period.

Finally we may draw attention to the frequent presence of elements of pure archi-tectural ornamentation—marble incrustations on the walls, friezes, festoons, imitations of hanging objects—which link up the last Etruscan tombs with the contemporary interior decoration of Hellenistic, Roman and Campanian houses.

BANQUET OF VELTHUR VELCHA. TOMB OF THE SHIELDS, TARQUINII.

TOMB OF THE SHIELDS

During the Hellenistic period the sepulchral hypogea continued to assume ever vaster proportions. They were built to receive several generations of members of the leading families of the Etruscan nobility, who now stood for the traditional glories of a civilization and a race on their decline. The Tomb of the Shields at Tarquinii belonged to the Velcha family. The paintings of the central chamber of the tomb were commissioned by Larth Velcha, who lived in the third century B.C. and held high rank in the priesthood. He is shown with his wife and ancestors in a sequence of pictures forming a sort of portrait gallery. The dead were perforce placed in the Underworld, but allusions to the infernal regions were discreet by kept down to the minimum.

The Velcha couples are feasting. Their heads crowned with wreaths and diadems, the ladies are reclining on couches strewn with embroidered cushions and rugs. They are resplendent in their jewels, and the atmosphere is one of ostentatious, extravagant opulence. The banqueters make the usual gestures, lightly touching each other, exchanging the ancient, conventional signs of affection. Yet, whether they are looking at one another or gazing into space, their faces convey a sense of brooding melancholy. From this eternal symposium, an exact replica of similar stately occasions in real life, there emanates a sense of superhuman weariness; the psychological ambiance is such that all these people gazing at us from the walls seem more like ghosts of a defunctive world than real men and women. We are shown Larth Velcha, who commissioned the decoration of the tomb, reclining on the banqueting couch in front of the well-spread table, while, according to the new custom, his wife, Velia Seitithi, sits beside him. She is gazing at him, and tenderly caresses his shoulder with her left hand, while with the other she proffers him an egg. Behind her a little slave girl holds up a feathered fan.

The names of the two chief characters are painted on the wall in huge letters behind their heads. Above the decoration runs a long untidy Etruscan inscription in praise of the noble lord Velcha, owner of the tomb. Here again the necessity of making clear the identity of the figures and pandering to the Velchas' family pride has led to a lapse of taste on the artist's part; he has mixed up scrawled inscriptions with delicately painted passages.

The pictures in the Tomb of the Shields are in fact one of the most revealing illustrations of Etruscan portraiture, and certainly the most important that has come down to us as regards the artists' technique. The practice of deliberately stressing all the elements capable of recalling the features of a given person, whether dead or alive, was not unknown to classical, and still prevailed in Hellenistic art. In Etruscan tomb painting, however, it catered for more specific and concrete exigencies, associated with the traditional magico-religious beliefs. Also that predilection for reality, for the specific and the anecdotal, which was for that matter one of the most characteristic traits in the art tradition of Etruscan painters, contributed to giving the Etruscan portrait its expressive power. Thus it was untouched by that tendency to harmony and idealization which we find in Greek portraiture, even during the Hellenistic period.

How far it is permissible, in the case of Etruscan portraiture, to speak of an absolute and total mastery of facial expression (as is true of Roman and, still more, of modern portraiture) is a moot point. However it is certain that even if in his portraits he was keeping to a schematic program then in current use, the artist who with a few brief strokes depicted Larth Velcha's intent, half-turned face, attempted, with every means at his disposal, to penetrate and to express the inmost being of the person he was called on to portray. In the terse, almost abstract handling of the majestic symmetry of the features, the forthright rendering of the scanty beard, the long slightly curving nose and the wide-open, dreamy eyes, we seem to see an attempt at introspection which, to the best of our knowledge, does not recur with anything like the same intensity until we come to the paintings and mosaics of Late Antiquity.

BANQUET OF LARTH VELCHA. TOMB OF THE SHIELDS, TARQUINII.

LARTH VELCHA'S MOTHER, DETAIL. TOMB OF THE SHIELDS, TARQUINII.

On another wall of the tomb we are shown Larth Velcha's parents, also taking part in a banquet. This scene is treated in almost the same spirit and with few variations. The two deceased members of the noble House are clad in white cloaks edged with black; the man, Velthur Velcha, holds the ceremonial *patera*; two musicians, a piper and a cithara-player, are approaching the festal couch, making their way with measured steps and fixed gaze through the grey dusk of the Underworld.

The portraits are solemn and reposeful, as in the other symposium. However, we find a very slight difference in the attitude of the figures, which undoubtedly had a psychological significance. In the banquet of Larth Velcha the lady is turning round to gaze at her illustrious husband, on whose portrait the artist seems to have concentrated his whole attention. Here the roles are interchanged. The man is looking at the lady, whose face, seen three-quarters, is exceptionally expressive. Can it be that, when ordering the decoration of the tomb, Larth Velcha wished above all to glorify the memory of a dearly loved mother ?

The figure of the dead woman, Ravnthu Aprthnai, is in any case one of the most interesting and stylistically most revealing paintings of the whole cycle of pictures in the Tomb of the Shields. The artist's conception and treatment of it calls for special attention. Generally speaking, the procedure employed in the painting of the figures of this tomb was still essentially the traditional one of outlining the forms and inner details, and filling in the zones thus demarcated with flat even color. Here and there, however, the artist makes attempts at chiaroscuro by the use of scumbles on bright surfaces, especially in the draperies and on the bare flesh of the women. The head of Ravnthu Aprthnai is a highly developed illustration of this technique, which was already widely diffused in classical painting. The contour line firmly demarcates the cheeks; but it also serves the function of chiaroscuro, by stressing the contrast between the brown of the right side of the face and the reddish hue of the left. It is emphasized by a brushstroke swerving inwards upon a tract of shadow formed by broken colors. The details of the nose, lips and chin are similarly treated. Light brown glazes accentuate the left cheek and the deep eye-sockets, while thick black brushstrokes indicate eye-brows, lids and irises. The hair and diadem are painted in masses of color, with shadings in the darker passages, telling out against the golden ground.

One tends to wonder if some more famous painter was not called in to make this portrait. However, this seems unlikely, since we find exactly the same methods of painting employed in some of the other portraits, especially the women. What is more likely is that the painter of the tomb took for his model an already existing portrait of the lady in the possession of the family, which had been painted by someone who was more versed in the procedures of contemporary Greek artists. (This would explain the difference between it and the other portraits, which are painted in the conventional manner.) In any case he achieved a quite original effect of quiet intensity in his rendering of the mournful, almost spectral face of the deceased lady. However, it cannot be denied that, when compared with that of Larth Velcha, this portrait shows less forcefulness of execution.

The walls of the Tomb of the Shields were covered with a vast array of paintings, but several of these are today in a sadly damaged state. There are both seated and standing figures, all of them doubtless members of the Velcha family to which we have already referred, or their kinsmen.

Particularly interesting is the little winged 'genius' above a small window to the right of the door at the back of the chamber, near the picture of Larth Velcha's banquet. He is engaged in writing on a open diptych (the type of book commonly used in the Hellenistico-Roman world). The Etruscan words inscribed on it record the fact that the embellishment of this tomb is due to Larth Velcha. Similarly placed, on the other side of the door, is another winged genius armed with two hammers. These two imaginary figures locate the paintings in the realm of the Underworld; this is also indicated by the murky haze—henceforth a conventional symbol of death—rising behind the banqueters. However, as already mentioned, these defunctive allusions are extremely discreet and not intended to convey any sense of terror. They, too, aim chiefly at extolling the high estate of the persons portrayed, and this indeed is the leitmotiv of the whole composition (as was announced by the little genius writing on the diptych). The artist who conceived the idea of the picture obviously drew his inspiration from the repertory of themes used in the figure-decoration of the Etruscan tombs of the second half of the fourth century. Similar banqueting scenes are to be found in the Tomb of Orcus and in the Golini Tombs near Orvieto. But it is obvious that the purport of these decorations had been completely changed as time went by. Thus here they serve merely as a pretext for the arrangement, i.e. the posing, of the figures, and are accessory to the leading theme, which is the portrait sequence.

The lack of co-ordination and uniformity in the technique is only one aspect of the evolution which was taking place in the art world of the Etruscans during the early Hellenistic period. In this particular case there are obvious anomalies in the painting. On the one hand we see a bold attempt to achieve expressive vigor based on principles of linear abstraction (Larth Velcha), and efforts are made to step up the general effect by the use of chiaroscuro (Ravnthu Aprthnai); on the other hand we find a painstaking, not to say servile copying of the exact appearance of persons and objects, resulting in a certain heaviness and even clumsiness. Here we certainly have the work of a second-rank artist, probably one who was trying to imitate the earlier, more successful achievements of painters who aimed at imparting expression to the portrait and exploiting the possibilities of chiaroscuro.

As regards the handling of colors, it should be noted that the painting in the Tomb of the Shields keeps to the four traditional colors, but employs them with an almost unlimited range of variations of intensity and a host of intermediary tones, obtained by mixing and diluting the pigments. The general chromatic effect is produced by gradations and variations of warm tints, with strong touches of black accentuating certain outlines and details. Noteworthy in this respect is the fine decorative quality of the big band of conventional black waves that runs along the dado bordering the figured frieze and making it tell out more strongly.

THE RULERS OF THE UNDERWORLD. TOMB OF ORCUS, TARQUINII.

TOMB OF ORCUS

The walls of the second chamber, also of very large dimensions, were decorated with a frieze dealing exclusively with the after-life in the world of the dead, which is depicted for the most part according to the Greek conception of Hades. Several sections of this frieze have survived. Possibly, following the usual practice, a banqueting scene was once appended and this was destroyed when the two tombs were joined together. But it is also possible that this frieze was painted precisely because of the enlargement of the first tomb, with a view to supplementing the picture sequence already existing in it. In any case the painting of the more recent frescos can be assigned to the third, or more probably to the second century B.C.

The scene depicting the life in the Underworld which figures on the walls of the last constructed chamber in the Tomb of Orcus is the most complete illustration that has come down to us of the art of classical antiquity. What we are shown is the Greek Hades, with its legendary denizens, each of them specified by name in the Etruscan inscriptions, and there are very few elements of local iconography. The depiction, or anyhow the greater part of it, of these type figures derives most probably from some classical prototype, perhaps the famous *Nekuia* (land of the dead) painted at Delphi by Polygnotos of Thasos.

On the wall which must have been the back wall as regards the original entrance to the sepulchre, we see the rulers of Hades seated on their thrones: Hades himself (or Pluto, also known as Orcus) and Persephone. The former is wearing a wolf-helmet and holding a snake in his left hand. Snakes are entwined in the hair of Persephone who is sumptuously attired and bejewelled. Facing the royal pair is a fully armed warrior with three heads, obviously the monster Geryon. The background is dappled with big white clouds standing out against a black sky. On the left, beside Geryon, are whitish rocks dotted with black, forming the entrance to a cavern, coming forth from which is a winged figure (in a rather bad state of preservation).

On the left wall is a row of figures alternating with dry, stylized plant forms; only parts of this frieze have survived. Starting from the left, we see first Ajax, then a venerable old man with ornate garments, hooded with a mantle and carrying a staff : the inscription describes him as " Souls of Tiresias." Some quaint diminutive figures, schematically drawn in black, are hopping about on a small tree beside him; these are probably *eidola* (simulacra of the dead) conjured up by the necromancer Tiresias. On the other side of the small tree stands a bearded man with curly hair, in a majestic attitude (we have a front view of him but his head is slightly turned); this is Agamemnon. He is wearing a cloak and a white scarf is knotted on his chest. Further to the left is a winged figure, few traces of which have survived.

On the wall beside the entrance, to the right of the original entrance, was another famous scene of the Underworld: the doom of Sisyphus. (Unfortunately this painting has gone badly to pieces.) Turning the corner, at the beginning of the right wall of the Tomb we come on a highly interesting scene, in a better state of preservation. Near a rock a young man, with long, flowing hair and a melancholy countenance, clad in a white himation which covers only half his body, is seated at a table, on the far side of which we glimpse another figure. The youth is stretching forth his arm; perhaps he is engaged in playing a game. (The inscription says this is the hero Theseus.) Meanwhile behind the table there looms up, apparently without the young man's seeing it, a horrific winged creature with the face of a bird of prey, asses' ears, and snakes rearing themselves above its head. The monster is brandishing threateningly a huge green serpent above the head of Theseus. This is the Etruscan demon Tuchulcha. The contrast between the comely young hero, unaware of the danger that is threatening him, and the hideousness of the infernal monster is one of the most tellingly emotive and brilliantly conceived effects in this remarkable *ensemble*.

THESEUS MENACED BY A DEMON, DETAIL. TOMB OF ORCUS, TARQUINII.

Just beyond the projection formed by the right wall of the tomb is a scene representing a winged demon and a young servant beside the table, made ready with an array of gold vases for the mystic banquet in the Underworld. These vases not only produce an impression of fabulous opulence but are arranged in a manner suggestive of a still life. In this detail (and indeed in all the elements of the scene) the artist has made a liberal use of chiaroscuro effects, obtaining these by transitional passages between tones, by the use of dots (in quite the pointillist manner) and apparent brushstrokes. But, while using these devices, he has kept to his structural technique of well-defined outlines and zones of uniform color, notably in the rendering of nudes and drapery. The color-scheme is exceptionally diversified and rich in nuances, ranging as it does from whites and blacks, the yellow of bright metals and the red of the men's flesh, to pink, orange-yellow, brown (in the hair), green in the non-human portions of the demons, grey, blue, iron-grey and purplish blue.

TABLE WITH PRECIOUS VESSELS. TOMB OF ORCUS, TARQUINII.

SACRIFICE OF THE TROJAN CAPTIVES. FRANÇOIS TOMB, VULCI.

FRANÇOIS TOMB

The François Tomb (which owes its name to the fact that it was discovered by the painter Alessandro François) contained some of the most impressive examples of Etruscan painting that exist; it is the only tomb in the Vulci necropolis that has escaped destruction. Most of the paintings were detached from the walls in 1862; the property of the Princes Torlonia, they are now in Rome. This tomb, which consists of several chambers, was built in the fifth century B.C., but the paintings, made for the Satie family, belong to the second or the beginning of the first century B.C. Covering the walls of the big central chamber, they consisted of a figured frieze illustrating episodes from Greek mythology, and local legends, and included portraits of real persons; there are also some elaborate decorative motifs. The walls of the back room are painted to imitate a revetment of marble slabs.

THE GODDESS VANTH, DETAIL. FRANÇOIS TOMB, VULCI.

THE DEMON CHARU, DETAIL. FRANÇOIS TOMB, VULCI.

The part of the frieze which occupied the walls on the left of the central chamber of the Tomb was composed of mythological scenes. Most of these derive from legends sanguinary in nature and depict heroes in the world of the Shades (as in the Nekuia of the Tomb of Orcus). However the scenes in the François Tomb are handled in a more episodic and narrative manner and it seems obvious that these compositions were inspired by motifs and methods of representation then prevailing in Greek art.

The largest picture, and the one which has come down to us in the best state of preservation, occupied the left wall at the back of the central chamber. It depicts a scene from the Iliad: the Trojan captives being sacrificed by Achilles at the tomb of Patroclus, his slain friend. Two of the Trojans are being thrust forward by the two heroes bearing the name Ajax, while the throat of another Trojan is being slit by Achilles, who is attended by two of the rulers of the Etruscan Underworld: Charu holding his hammer and the goddess Vanth with outspread wings. On the left " the soul of Patroclus," in the guise of a comely youth wrapped in a cloak with a white band across his chest, is watching the scene, as is Agamemnon, a man of royal mien and regally attired. The structure of the composition and the grouping of the figures derive from an original Greek version of the Homeric episode, though they also speak for the artist's mature experience. For there is no doubt that this picture echoes some lost Greek composition, probably belonging to the fourth century B.C. or the early phase of Hellenism, imitations of which can also be seen in other Etruscan monuments.

However, the stylistic and technical qualities of this work cannot be due solely to the imitation, however skillful, of some famous prototype. The personal talent and culture of the Etruscan painter are unmistakable both in his over-all handling of the composition and in the adroitness with which he has intercalated the figures of Vanth and Charu, fantastic denizens of the Etruscan Underworld making an unlook-ed-for appearance among the heroes of the ancient legend of Troy. Far from giving the impression of an anachronism, they heighten the dramatic tension of the scene both in its psychological effect and in its artistic presentation. There is something at once infinitely noble and sternly inexorable—the virginal beauty of an angel of death— in this picture of Vanth, the Etruscan goddess of destiny, spreading her vast wings as though to enclasp in a like imminence of tragedy the sad shade of Patroclus and the savage wrath of Achilles. On the other side stands Charu, a gaunt, livid blue, scowling figure waiting to carry off the soul of the nameless, innocent victim, but gazing in front of him as if he foresaw the doom of the hero Achilles himself and were gloating over his future prey. The faces of these two strange beings are among the finest achievements of Etruscan painting. In contrast with the strong relief imparted by the chiaroscuro to the other figures, their bodies are portrayed chiefly by way of drawing and color.

On other sectors of the walls, with occasional breaks of continuity due to the side doors, were painted the following scenes: the fight between Eteocles and Polynices, Nestor and Phoenix, each before a palmtree, and Cassandra slain by Ajax. On the other side of the entrance door, on the right, was painted the punishment of Sisyphus, watched by Amphiaraus. But only a few fragments of these paintings have survived.

FIGHT BETWEEN ETEOCLES AND POLYNICES. FRANÇOIS TOMB, VULCI.

On the right-hand party wall between the large room and the inner chamber, and encroaching on the adjoining walls for a short distance, there was a picture sequence whose subject-matter, of local type and derived from Etruscan legends, is for various reasons of quite exceptional interest. This set of pictures, happily in a good state of preservation, serves as a pendant to the scene of the sacrifice of the Trojan captives, and represents male figures, naked, cloaked or wearing armor, arranged in couples. All these scenes are concerned with fighting. In the first, beginning from the left, we are shown a warrior (whose name—Caile Vipinas—figures in the inscription) being liberated by another warrior, named Macstrna. Then come four pairs of combatants, one of whom is always shown succumbing to the other's onslaught. The name and birthplace of each vanquished man are written in, and one of these names is of much interest: Cneve Tarchunies Rumach, i.e. Gnaeus Tarquinius of Rome. One of the victors is named Avle Vipinas. Here we have certainly an historical scene, depicting the exploits of the Etruscan heroes Mastarna, Caelius and Aulus Vibenna. The last two named were brothers hailing from Vulci and an old historical tradition associates them with the Kings of Rome. Probably this scene relates to a victory of these early condottieri over the warriors or rulers of certain Etruscan cities and Rome herself, in the days of the Tarquin Kings. Since the Vibenna (or Vipina) brothers came from Vulci we have good reason for believing that the paintings in the François Tomb were intended to celebrate the glorious past of the city of Vulci. Though individual figures owe something to Greek models, the composition of this battlepiece is strikingly original. It says much for the genius of the artist that he has so brilliantly diversified the attitudes, movements and expressions of his figures.

The artist's ability is no less manifest in the portraits on the right-hand side wall of the sepulchral chamber. (An interesting point is that this wall surface was made available by blocking up a door which originally led into one of the side-chambers.) There are three figures, all standing: two men and a woman. Only in the case of the first male figure, who is attended by a small page, is the entire painting intact. He is a young man with short black hair and his name is given as Vel Satie. A wreath of small leaves encircles his head and his body is wrapped in a voluminous purplish-blue cloak, the edges of which are embroidered with a scroll-work pattern and the rest of it painted with figures; this, in fact, is a handsome specimen of the " toga pincta." He wears shoes of yellow cloth or leather. Beside him squats an obese little dwarf wearing a white dark-edged tunic and on his left hand is perched a tethered bird, doubtless a bantam hunting hawk.

Here we have the only portrait—full-length and posed with an eye to dignified effects—that has come down to us from classical antiquity prior to the advent of the Roman Empire. In the rendering of his model the artist displays a feeling for style bordering on virtuosity. The features are markedly individual, while the half-parted lips and the upturned eyes convey a sense of meditation, tinged with melancholy. The firmness of the linework, the handling of the patches of color, and the chiaroscuro combine to build up an effect of fully modeled plastic form.

PORTRAIT OF VEL SATIE. FRANÇOIS TOMB, VULCI.

ANIMAL FRIEZE, DETAIL. FRANÇOIS TOMB, VULCI.

Above the large fresco and the doors ran a small animal frieze which contains a varied assortment of animals, indigenous and exotic: horses, dogs, boars, bulls, lions, panthers and other felines; also griffins and a snake. These are depicted either separately and usually running, or else in groups of twos and threes with wild beasts in the act of pouncing on other animals. The subjects in question, which appear in other Etruscan decorations, are here rendered with vivacity and delicacy, and also with a touch of archaism.

Whether appraised on the basis of their subject-matter or of the style as a whole, the decorations in the François Tomb point to a diversity of influences. In fact we should almost be justified in speaking of eclecticism, were it not that the artist, obviously a strong personality, has so successfully integrated his various sources, welding the imported elements together and at the same time imposing on them the imprint of his personal gifts for invention and expression. This holds good especially for the battle scene (whose subject-matter is Etruscan) and for the portrait of Vel Satie, anyhow for what can still be seen of it. It is a matter for regret that neither the name of this artist has come down to us, nor those of such other fine painters of more ancient times as the Master of the Tomb of the Triclinium.

ANIMAL FRIEZE, DETAIL. FRANÇOIS TOMB, VULCI.

Fixing the chronology of these paintings is a problem inseparable from that of the cultural background of the artist himself, who in choosing and arranging the subjects of his frieze certainly kept to a program enjoined by well-established traditions of funerary art, and perhaps also by the wishes of those commissioning the tomb. Though such works were chiefly intended to commemorate the dead in all their glory and also to conjure up visions of the Other World, the pictures in the François Tomb on the whole spare us that sinister Baroque depiction of Avernus, featuring its horrors with grim precision, which we so often find in Etruscan tomb painting of the Hellenistic period. Here, on the contrary, the Underworld is discreetly, indirectly evoked in terms of mythological allusions. The painter set out to picture the violent death and tragic destiny of certain legendary heroes; but beside these famous Greek figures he also saw fit to include the more modest heroes of local tradition, in a spirit of discursive erudition that might almost be described as " Varronian."

As against the generally accepted view that this tomb belongs to the end of the fourth or the beginning of the third century, more recent opinion would situate it in the late Hellenistic period. The choice of subjects supports this dating, which is rendered even more plausible by a study of the ornamental motifs and above all of the illusionist architectural lay-out of the revetment of the inner chamber, recalling that of the decorative motifs in the painting of the so-called " second style " at Pompeii. The fact is that even in the graphic procedures of the small animal frieze we find echoes of classicist art. Both the proportions and the imposing presentation of the large frieze link it closely with the so-called " megalographies," which did not come into fashion until about the same time as the " second style," i.e. during the first half of the first century B.C. And just as this great decorative painting gave new life on Italian soil to the time-honored themes of Greek art, so did the painter of the François Tomb avail himself of Greek models not for the purpose of mere imitation, but as a basis upon which his own genius could build. We have one example among many in the scene depicting the sacrifice of the Trojan captives, whose style and tone are set above all by the figures of Vanth and Charu. Moreover, both the facial expressions and the technical methods employed in rendering the Greek myth seem to bear a common stamp; this we can see in the portrait of Vel Satie and in the legendary Etruscan scenes, even though the chiaroscuro and the color effects are sometimes deliberately exaggerated.

ANIMAL FRIEZE, DETAIL. FRANÇOIS TOMB, VULCI.

PROCESSION TO THE OTHER WORLD, DETAIL. TOMB OF THE TYPHON, TARQUINII.

TOMB OF THE TYPHON

The Tomb of the Typhon is a large aristocratic tomb at Tarquinii, originally owned by the noble family bearing the name of Pumpu. It contains a central pilaster and ledges along the walls on which the sarcophagi were placed. The paintings in it were probably made in the first century B.C. Thus it may be regarded as the last achievement of Etruscan painting which has come down to us in a sufficiently good state of preservation to enable its critical appraisal.

The large wall-surface available in this tomb was only partially adorned with painting. The quadrangular stone pilaster left in the center of the tomb for structural reasons has a molded cornice painted with the egg-and-dart pattern, an ogee and dentils, and, below, a strip of rosettes. The dedicatory inscription is recorded on the back of the pilaster. On the sides are two identical figures of winged giants whose legs terminate in snakes, the so-called " typhons " which have given this tomb its name. On the remaining face of the pilaster is a stylized, archaistic female figure clad in drapery whose folds end in volutes. Also, we find traces of a scene (damaged almost out of recognition) painted on the surface of a mass of rock shaped as a parallelopiped, placed just in front of the pilaster and forming a sort of console. At the top of the wall, above the several tiers, runs a decorative band painted in red and black upon the white plaster. It is divided up as follows: beginning from its lower edge, we have first a series of dentils, then a row of rosettes and finally a line of stylized waves amongst which dolphins are leaping. This decorative motif is interrupted only in the middle of the right wall, where it gives place to a full-size picture. This shows figures clad in togas, members of the Pumpu family, as the inscription informs us. It would seem that they are being escorted to the World of the Shades by monstrous demons having the attributes of that grim Etruscan deity Charun.

The best preserved paintings are those on the pilaster. On its left side we have the Typhon, his stalwart body rendered with extremely free and bold foreshortenings; his legs are splayed out and he is shoring himself up on his knees. The strain of bearing a huge weight that taxes all his strength on his uplifted arms is vividly conveyed. He is leaning a little forward, towards the left, as though watching something intently. His head is shown full-face, his arms are outstretched and his hands are pressed flat against the cornice, holding it up. A black contour-line circumscribes his body, whose bulging muscularity is plastically rendered by the play of chiaroscuro in the over-all brick-red tonality. This is softened down by scumbles of broken colors in the highlights until it merges into the pale pink of the fully illuminated areas. Some dark brown lines stress the reliefs of the chiaroscuro (in the Typhon's groin, the folds of his abdomen, the *linea alba*, the pectoral muscles). The non-human portions of this hybrid being are painted in blue-grey. From the knee downwards his limbs change into writhing snakes, in which we find, as in the patches indicating scales, the same handling of chiaroscuro as in the body. The head of the snake on the left is clearly indicated. Behind the monster's shoulders are huge wings whose modeling and details are rendered by passages of light and dark blue-grey, modulating into white. We find the same tonalities in the upstanding shock of curly hair, whereas the hair falling on the shoulders is indicated by black brushstrokes. The Typhon's face, which most regrettably is in a bad state of preservation, was doubtless intended to convey the tension and passion on which the Hellenistic artists set such store; we see hints of this in the staring eyes and the high, strongly curved superciliary arches. The female figure on the back of the pilaster is painted entirely in blue-grey, and with the same technique as that used for the giants' wings.

Though they have " monstrous " aspects associating them with the iconography of Etruscan funerary painting of the late period, the function of the motifs on the pilasters is essentially decorative. The inspiration behind motifs of this kind was typically

GIANT WITH SERPENT-LEGS. TOMB OF THE TYPHON, TARQUINII.

Greek and Hellenistic, and the resemblances between the Typhons and the Giants with anguiform limbs of the Great Altar of Pergamum are plain to see. However, it is highly probable that these themes came to have a place in the repertory of the decorator of the Tomb of the Typhon not directly, but by way of a long series of pictures of similar subjects deriving from unknown prototypes representing giants holding up the sky. These, in their turn, probably derived from Asiatic art, from Pergamum or Rhodes. Also the general lay-out, the dynamic tension and plastic fullness of the bodies tend to show that these Typhons owe much to that background of Asiatic Hellenism which had so much influence on contemporary Etruscan sculpture.

That this work was at once derivative and in its way a new creation is evidenced also by the woman's figure on the back of the pilaster. Its archaizing and decorative compositional scheme and the monochrome painting clearly point to classicist inspiration, a far cry from the style of Asiatic art, and to sources whose diffusion was comparatively recent. Though the giants may be ascribed to the first half of the second century B.C., the female figure belongs to a type of decoration which cannot be dated earlier than the end of the second or the beginning of the first century.

The figures on the pilaster have an ornamental and eclectic character directly opposed to the manner in which the scene on the right-hand wall of the tomb is painted. In the latter we are back in a world that is typically Etruscan, and the sense of irremediable loss, the anguish of bereavement, is expressed with an intensity rarely found in other funerary works of art. Indeed this feeling of grief seems to overrule the original purpose of these paintings: to commemorate and glorify the dead. Yet the persons buried here were surely eminent, amongst them being Laris Pumpu (perhaps the builder of this tomb) whom the inscription describes as being of priestly rank. A group of men in white togas, followed by one or two women, are being driven forward by a horde of hideous demons carrying torches, hammers and musical instruments.

What is most interesting in this picture (unhappily in very poor condition) is not its technique, which seems less skillful than that of the Typhon and in any case is very different from it. What strikes us here is the great variety of figures, seen in profile or three-quarters face, the tense expression of the features and in particular the way in which the individual structure of the faces is made to blend into a sort of crowd-effect. To this end illusionist devices are employed; heads are arranged in tiers and profiles superimposed, while the lines of the garments touch and even tend to intersect each other. All these characteristics link up the decorations in the Tomb of the Typhon with certain Roman paintings and especially bas-reliefs dealing with realistic and historical subjects, such as the processional frieze of the Ara Pacis of Augustus. This confirms the ascription of these decorations to the first century B.C., perhaps even to its latter half. They also have historical value as illustrating the transition from Etruscan art traditions to Roman art.

MAP OF ETRURIA

This map shows the principal Etruscan
towns and also smaller towns in which
painted monuments have been discovered.
The names are given in Latin with the
modern names below, in parentheses.
The greater modern towns are located
by circles.

CHRONOLOGICAL TABLE

WITH A LIST OF THE CHIEF MONUMENTS OF ETRUSCAN PAINTING

In the first column are listed the monuments of Etruscan painting, those not described and illustrated in the present volume being in italics. The second column contains a brief indication of the most important events and orientations of the contemporary artistic culture. The third column gives the approximate dates.

	Flowering of the " orientalizing " trend of art in Central Italy—First direct artistic influences of the Greek world on Etruria (traditions concerning the coming of artists in the company of Damaratus of Corinth: Pliny, XXXV, 152)—Protocorinthian, Palaeo-Corinthian and Rhodian pottery diffused in Italy.	Ca. 650-600 B.C.
Tombs of the Painted Lions and of the Painted Animals, Caere.		
Campana Tomb, Veii.	Doric, chiefly Corinthian, art trends in Etruria—Last phase of the "orientalizing" culture—Contacts with Greek colonies of Southern Italy, voyages of East Greeks in the Western seas: hence first Ionic influences.	Ca. 600-550.
Boccanera slabs, Caere.		
Tomb of the Bulls, Tarquinii. *Tomb of the Inscriptions, Tarquinii.* Campana slabs, Caere. Tomb of the Augurs, Tarquinii. *Tomb of the Dead Man, Tarquinii.* Tomb of the Lionesses, Tarquinii.	Direct influence of East Greek art trends in Etruria, and probable immigration of East Greek artists: Caeretan *hydriai*—Economic and artistic apogee of the towns in Southern Etruria—Ionic and Attic black-figured vases diffused in Italy.	Ca. 550-520.
Tomb of Hunting and Fishing, Tarquinii. Tomb of the Bacchants, Tarquinii. *Tombs of the Old Man and of the Painted Vases, Tarquinii.* Tomb of the Baron, Tarquinii. *Tomb of the Dying Man, Tarquinii.*	Triumph of the Ionico-Etruscan style in its fully developed phase: painting in Tarquinii, metal-work in Vulci and Perugia, terracotta modeling in Veii (the Master of the Apollo) —Attic red-figured vases of the most ancient style diffused in Italy—Innovations in drawing; foreshortenings attributed to Kimon of Cleonae.	520-490.
Tomb of the Chariots, Tarquinii. *Tomb of the Citharoedus, Tarquinii.* *Tomb of Orpheus and Eurydice, Chiusi.* Tomb of the Monkey, Chiusi. *Slabs of Veii.* Tomb of the Leopards, Tarquinii.	Influence of Attic art in Etruria; Attic red-figured vases of the late archaic and transitional style diffused in Italy—Decline of the towns in Southern Etruria and cultural and artistic ascendancy of Chiusi.	490-470.

Tomb of the Triclinium, Tarquinii. Tomb of the Funeral Couch, Tarquinii. *Tomb of the Hill, Chiusi.* Francesca Giustiniani Tomb, Tarquinii. *Querciola Tomb, Tarquinii.* *Tomb della Pulcella, Tarquinii.* *Paolozzi Tomb, Chiusi.*	Establishment of Classical art in Greece: painting of Polygnotos, Mikon, Panainos, Zeuxis, Parrhasios; perspective and chiaroscuro—Limited diffusion of Greek red-figured pottery of Classical style—" Sub-archaic " phase in Etruria with persistence of archaic motifs and slight penetration of Classical influences—General decadence of the Etruscan world.	470-400.
Sarcophagus of the Amazons, Tarquinii.	Further development of Classical art in Greece: problems of the expression of feelings; painting of Nikomachos, Philoxenos *et al.*—Flowering of painted pottery in the Greek towns of Southern Italy—Classical influence penetrates Etruria directly and indirectly (*via* Southern Italy).	Ca. 400-340.
Golini Tombs, Orvieto. Tomb of Orcus (earlier chamber), Tarquinii.	Rise of Hellenistic painting in Greece: Apelles, Antiphilos, Theon *et al.*—Artistic activity revives in Central Italy—Etruria submits to Roman hegemony.	Ca. 340-280.
Tomb of the Shields, Tarquinii. *Bruschi Tomb, Tarquinii.*	Hellenistic art (schools of painting at Rhodes, Pergamum, Alexandria), its influence in Italy—" Baroque " trends and expressionistic tendencies; flowering of the Etruscan portrait—Apogee of the towns in Northern Etruria.	Ca. 280-150.
Tomb of Orcus (later chamber), Tarquinii. *Tomb of the Cardinal, Tarquinii.* *Campanari Tomb, Vulci.* François Tomb, Vulci. Tomb of the Typhon, Tarquinii.	Diffusion of classicist art trends—A uniform culture progressively establishes itself in Italy—Decorative painting of " first " and " second style ": megalography.	Ca. 150-30 B.C.

The following minor corrections in the text should be noted : for " Magliana " page 9 line 40 read " Magliano " ; for " Sicyonia " page 25 line 4 read " Sicyon " ; for " southern Asiatic Ionia " page 46 line 25 read " northern Asiatic Ionia " ; for " imported directly from the cultural centers of Magna Graecia " page 91 line 67 read " imported directly or indirectly from the cultural centers of Magna Graecia " ; for " Hellenistic " page 91 line 9 read " Hellenic ".

NOTE ON THE NOMENCLATURE
OF THE PAINTED TOMBS

The painted tombs at Tarquinii, Chiusi, Orvieto, Vulci, Caere and Veii are usually designated by conventional names, often of a quaint or picturesque nature, which seem to call for some words of explanation. When they were discovered the attention of the first visitors and illustrators was caught by some striking detail, and this was the origin of the names—of a makeshift, somewhat trivial order and sometimes, indeed, incorrect, so far as the real significance of the figures is concerned—which have entered not only into common usage but also into scientific terminology. Of this type are such names as those of the Tombs of the Augurs, of the Lionesses, of Hunting and Fishing, of the Chariots, of the Monkey, of the Triclinium, of the Shields etc. In other cases tombs were named after their discoverers or some famous visitor—e.g. the Campana Tomb, the François Tomb, the Tomb of the Baron, the Francesca Giustiniani Tomb, the Golini Tomb.

In guide-books for tourists and in the literature of archaeology these tombs are commonly referred to under their original Italian names. With a view to enabling our readers more readily to locate references to these tombs in other books, and also to helping those who decide to visit the tombs to find their way about more easily, we join hereunder a list of the traditional Italian names and their English equivalents, set out in alphabetical order in parallel columns. (In this list are not included tombs which are designated by names of persons.)

Animali Dipinti	Painted Animals
Auguri	Augurs
Baccanti	Bacchants
Barone	Baron
Bighe	Chariots
Caccia e Pesca	Hunting and Fishing
Cardinale	Cardinal
Citaredo	Citharoedus
Colle (o Due Bighe)	Hill (or Two Chariots)
Iscrizioni	Inscriptions
Leonesse	Lionesses
Leoni Dipinti	Painted Lions
Leopardi	Leopards
Letto Funebre	Funeral Couch
Morente	Dying Man
Morto	Dead Man
Orco	Orcus
Orfeo e Euridice	Orpheus and Eurydice
Pulcinella	Punchinello
Scimmia	Monkey
Scudi	Shields
Tifone	Typhon
Tori	Bulls
Triclinio	Triclinium
Vasi Dipinti	Painted Vases
Vecchio	Old Man

BIBLIOGRAPHY

ETRUSCAN ART

MARTHA, J. *L'art étrusque*. Paris 1889.

DUCATI, P. *Storia dell'arte etrusca*. Florence 1927.

GIGLIOLI, G. Q. *L'arte etrusca*. Milan 1935.

ANCIENT PAINTING

PFUHL, E. *Malerei und Zeichnung der Griechen*. Munich 1923.

SWINDLER, M. H. *Ancient Painting, from the Earliest Times to the Period of Christian Art*. London, Oxford 1929.

DUCATI, P. *Pittura etrusca italo-greca e romana*. Novara 1941. (Also published in French.)

MONOGRAPHS AND STUDIES OF ETRUSCAN PAINTING

1. GENERAL :

WEEGE, F. *Etruskische Malerei*. Halle 1921.

POULSEN, F. *Etruscan Tomb Paintings, their Subjects and Significance*. Oxford 1922.

NEPPI MODONA, A. *Pittura etrusca*, in " Historia," IV, 1930, p. 96 ff.

2. ARCHAIC PAINTING :

MESSERSCHMIDT, F. *Beiträge zur Chronologie der etruskischen Wandmalerei*. I, *Die archaische Zeit*, Halle 1928.

BOVINI, G. *La pintura etrusca del período orientalizante (siglos VII y VI a. de J. C.)*, in " Ampurias," XI, 1949, p. 63 ff.

3. PAINTING FOURTH-FIRST CENTURY B.C. :

NEPPI MODONA, A. *Di alcuni problemi suggeriti dalla pittura etrusca del IV-II secolo*, in " Annali delle Università Toscane," X, 1926, p. 223 ff.

MESSERSCHMIDT, F. *Probleme der etruskischen Malerei des Hellenismus*, in " Jahrbuch des Deutschen Archäologischen Instituts," XLV, 1930, p. 62 ff.

4. GENERAL PURPORT :

PALLOTTINO, M. *Partecipazione e senso drammatico nel mondo figurativo degli Etruschi*, in " Arti Figurative," III-V, 1946, p. 149 ff.

5. TECHNICAL STUDIES :

DE WIT, J. *Die Vorritzungen der etruskischen Grabmalerei*, in " Jahrbuch des Deutschen Archäologischen Instituts," XLIV, 1929, p. 31 ff.

BRANZANI, L. *Le pitture murali degli Etruschi. Osservazioni sulla loro tecnica*, in " Studi Etruschi," VII, 1933, p. 335 ff.

CAGIANO DE AZEVEDO, M. *Il distacco delle pitture della tomba delle Bighe*, in " Bollettino dell'Istituto Centrale del Restauro," 2, 1950.

CAGIANO DE AZEVEDO, M. *Il distacco delle pitture della tomba del Triclinio*, in " Bollettino dell'Istituto Centrale del Restauro," 3-4, 1951.

BIBLIOGRAPHY OF THE MONUMENTS BY SITES

1. PAINTINGS AT CAERE :

MENGARELLI, R. *Caere e le recenti scoperte*, in " Studi Etruschi," I, 1927, p. 145 ff.

NEPPI MODONA, A. *Pitture etrusche arcaiche. Le lastre fittili policrome ceretane*, in " Emporium," 1928, p. 97 ff.

2. PAINTINGS AT CHIUSI :

BIANCHI BANDINELLI, R. *Clusium*, in " Monumenti Antichi dei Lincei," XXX, 1925.

BIANCHI BANDINELLI, R. *Clusium. Le pitture delle tombe arcaiche (Monumenti della pittura antica scoperti in Italia)*. Rome 1939.

3. PAINTINGS AT ORVIETO :

MARELLA VIANELLO, M. *Si puo parlare di scuola orvietana e di tradizione locale orvietana nella storia della pittura sepolcrale degli Etruschi ?* in " Antichità," I, 1947, p. 1 ff.

4. PAINTINGS AT TARQUINII :

BULLE, H. *Die Malerschule von Tarquini*, in " Kunst und Künstler," XX, 1921-22, p. 378 ff.

DUELL, P. *The Tomba del Triclinio at Tarquinia*, in " Memoirs of the American Academy at Rome," VII, 1927, p. 47 ff.

PALLOTTINO, M. *Tarquinia*, in " Monumenti Antichi dei Lincei," XXXVI, 1937.

DUCATI, P. *Tarquinii. Le pitture delle tombe delle Leonesse e dei Vasi Dipinti (Monumenti della pittura antica scoperti in Italia)*. Rome 1937.

ROMANELLI, P. *Tarquinii. Le pitture della tomba della Caccia e della Pesca (Monumenti della pittura antica scoperti in Italia)*. Rome, 1938.

DUCATI, P. *Osservazioni cronologiche sulle pitture arcaiche etrusche*, in " Studi Etruschi," XIII, 1939, p. 203 ff.

ROMANELLI, P. *Tarquinia. La necropoli e il museo (Itinerari dei Musei e Monumenti d'Italia)*. Rome 1940.

CAGIANO DE AZEVEDO, M. *Alcuni punti oscuri della nostra critica circa la pittura etrusca del VI e V secolo a.C.*, in " Archeologia Classica," II, 1950, p. 59 ff.

Individual references to other tombs and to painted objects are given in the work mentioned above : PALLOTTINO, *Tarquinia*, columns 296 ff. and 401 ff.

5. PAINTINGS AT VEII :

RUMPF, A. *Die Wandmalereien in Veii*. Leipzig 1915.

STEFANI, E. *Una serie di lastre fittili dipinte del santuario etrusco di Veio*, in " Archeologia Classica," III, 1951, p. 138 ff.

6. PAINTINGS AT VULCI :

MESSERSCHMIDT, F. *Nekropolen von Vulci*. Berlin 1930.

For an attempt to ascribe the painted decorations of the François Tomb to the late Hellenistic period, see : A. VON GERKAN in " Mitteilungen des Deutschen Archäologischen Instituts. Römische Abteilung," LVII, 1942, p. 146 ff.

For the inscriptions in painted tombs the Corpus Inscriptionum Etruscarum, *vol. II, sect. 1, fasc. 1, 2, 3, Leipzig, may be consulted.*

INDEX OF MONUMENTS BY SITES AND MUSEUMS

The page-numbers in italics refer to the illustrated chapters in which the painted monuments are discussed at length.

INDEX OF NAMES AND SUBJECTS

CONTENTS

THE COLORPLATES

On the jacket figures a detail of the Conversation Piece (Tomb of the Baron, Tarquinii) *of page 58.*

THIS VOLUME OF THE COLLECTION

THE GREAT CENTURIES OF PAINTING

WAS PRINTED

BOTH TEXT AND COLORPLATES

BY THE

SKIRA

COLOR STUDIO

AT IMPRIMERIES RÉUNIES S. A.

LAUSANNE

FINISHED THE THIRTIETH DAY OF SEPTEMBER

NINETEEN HUNDRED AND FIFTY-TWO

*All the work produced by the Skira Color Studio
is carried out by the technical staff of
Editions d'Art Albert Skira*

PRINTED IN SWITZERLAND